# BROKEN LINES

AN ILLUSTRATED NOVEL

*by*

Tom Pappalardo

COPYRIGHT 2018
Tom Pappalardo
Object Publishing

ISBN 978-0-9983278-1-5

BROKEN-LINES.COM

This low-priced Object Publishing Book has been completely reset in Husqvarna Condensed Extra Wide, a type face designed for easy reading, and was printed from new plates. It contains the complete text of the original hard-cover edition.
NOT ONE WORD HAS BEEN OMITTED.

"This book was written on Foster's Lager, Budweiser, Bombay Gin, lots of Jack Daniels, Kahlua and Brandy, Quackers and Krell, and Wild Women!"

BY TOM PAPPALARDO

*One More Cup Of Coffee*

*Everything You Didn't Ask For*

*Failure, Incompetence*

*Through The Wood, Beneath The Moon*
(with Matt Smith)

*Fictitious! Exaggerate Your Accomplishments With Fake Book Titles*

*Call Of The Wild: A Book Report*

To

# THE MILLIONS

WHO WOULD, AND MAY,

## 𝕰𝖆𝖘𝖎𝖑𝖞 𝖆𝖓𝖉 𝕲𝖗𝖆𝖈𝖊𝖋𝖚𝖑𝖑𝖞 𝕰𝖝𝖕𝖗𝖊𝖘𝖘 𝖙𝖍𝖊 𝕽𝖎𝖌𝖍𝖙 𝕿𝖍𝖔𝖚𝖌𝖍𝖙

THIS WORK IS

## RESPECTFULLY DEDICATED.

# LIST OF ILLUSTRATIONS

# LIST OF ILLUSTRATIONS

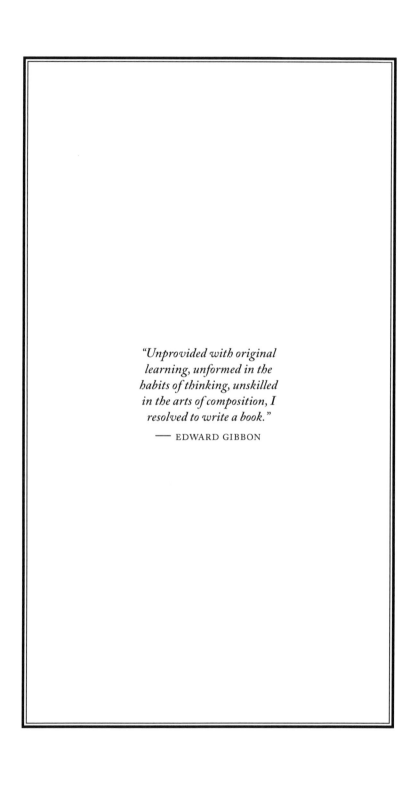

"Unprovided with original learning, unformed in the habits of thinking, unskilled in the arts of composition, I resolved to write a book."

—— EDWARD GIBBON

# PART ONE
## Fire & Coffee

IN WHICH OUR HEROES ARE
INTRODUCED AND PLOTTY THINGS
ARE ESTABLISHED

"EVIL"

# AN EMBARRASSMENT OF THREE-RING BINDERS

"Coffeee time!" the demon sings.

"Put it there, Henry" his boss says. The demon places the coffee mug on a filing cabinet by the door and leans against the jamb. Henry doesn't know why the Chief always asks for coffee. He never drinks it. The demon taps his foot to a song that's been stuck in his hollow black head for days. Don't let the name of the song concern you. It doesn't affect the plot in any way.

The Chief sits on the corner of his desk. He looks brittle and worn. "Henry," he says after twenty seconds of silence. "Bring me the telephone book."

"No one uses those anymore, Chief."

"Henry. Bring me the telephone book."

The demon shuffles into the office, his ill-fitting rubber boots squeaking on the tile floor. He is dressed as a fireman. All of the demons are. They are Firemen.

The Chief's office reminds Henry of a high school guidance counselor's office. The old Steelcase desk is beige and scuffed, flanked by several filing cabinets, drawers half-open. Piles of Department paperwork teeter on every surface, though the Chief isn't much of a reader, at least as far as Henry knows. The cinderblock walls are dirty and drab, a horizontal line at eye level separating an indeterminable darker color from an indescribable lighter one.

"Where'd you leave it, Chief?" Henry asks.

"It's there, under those binders."

Henry wades into the mound of three-ring binders and dives below the surface. A moment later he leaps out, a telephone book held high.

"Boo-yah!"

"Open it and pick a place," the Chief instructs.

Henry giddily does as he is told. He looks away as he

points a finger towards the open book, adding a needless flourish to his wrist movement. "Aspirational Heights Economy Living," he announces. "I think it's a trailer park."

"Wonderful," the Chief sighs. "Gather some of the boys. Burn the buildings, burn the people, spread fear."

"Evil!" Henry enthuses. "You got it!" He slaps the telephone book shut and lets it drop to the floor. "Leave no stone unburned, right, Chief?"

"I told you to stop saying that. It doesn't make any sense."

"No prob, Chief!" Henry salutes and hustles out the door.

"No prob," the Chief mutters to the empty office.


# KICKERS

THE WAITRESS IS ON AUTOPILOT, moving mechanically through the near-empty 'Kickers 24/7 Family Pub and Sports Bar. Refill sugar, refill salt, refill pepper, dump half-and-half. Wipe down the surfaces, wipe down the drink machines, wipe down the booth seats. Windex the framed faux-vintage photos hanging on the walls, dust the pop culture memorabilia bolted to the bar. She organizes the menus and picks bits of lettuce off the floor. Eight and a half hours into her shift, and Maggie is trying her best to stay occupied and awake.

*"We are what we repeatedly do."*
— ARISTOTLE

Big snow fell overnight and business has been slow. As the sun reveals itself over the 'Kickers parking lot, two snow plow guys sit in the big window booth, bleary-eyed and exhausted, under a wall-mounted guitar autographed by Steve Vai. Duffy and Kev stare at the closest of the nine flat screen TVs in silence. Local news. "Sweet Caroline" plays from unseen speakers, muffled by the ceiling tiles, passing through the heater vents, propelled forward by the air conditioners, reflected off the tile floors, and absorbed by the cheap carpeting. The song creeps into the booths, the walk-in freezer, the drains and pipes. The line cook hums it. Maggie taps a finger against the side of the cash register to the beat. The plow guys begin an idle argument, unable to agree on who they're listening to. Neil Diamond, says Duffy; Kev thinks it's Barry Manilow. Neither man is awake enough to argue his point or look it up on Wikipedia.*

The only other customers in the restaurant — a cowboy and a spaceman — sit in the back booth. The cowboy chews on a wooden coffee stirrer (he's been trying to quit smoking and it's the only thing preventing him from punching his little companion). The spaceman is constructing a small tower of Smuckers jelly packs, a prime example of the sort of thing that might cause the cowboy to punch him.

"We're gonna need chains for the tires, I reckon," the cowboy says.

"Because of the snow?" the spaceman asks.

Cowboy's whole face pinches inward. "Yes, because of the f██king snow. Why the f██k else would we—?" He closes his eyes and massages his temples. "I mean, what the f██k is wrong with you?"

"Too much sassafras?" the spaceman ventures.

"Hey! No fights in my section," Maggie jokes as she approaches the table.

"Sorry, ma'am. Sometimes the little fella makes me so angry I could just about bite myself, is all."

She eyes the Cowboy's revolver strapped to his thigh. "Keep 'em holstered."

"Will do."

"All righty then. Your meatloaf okay?"

"Real fine, ma'am," The cowboy nods. It's terrible.

"How about your pancakes?" she asks the spaceman.

---

* They're actually listening to Frank Sinatra's jaunty big band interpretation from his 1974 album *Some Nice Things I've Missed*.

Double thumbs-up. His plate is empty. She wants to ask how he managed to eat a large stack of pancakes with a glass dome fully encasing his head, but she senses this line of questioning and the ensuing explanation would aggravate his cowboy friend.

Maggie smiles and nods and walks away because that's part of the job. She's a waitress, goddamnit.

———⊸◦◖∅◗◦⊶———

MAGGIE HAULS THE GIANT JUG OF KETCHUP out from under the conveyor toaster. The line cook slouches on a barstool, staring at the muted TV above the door. Two more fires this week. The local news stations have dubbed it "The Winter Of Fire." It has its own logo and dramatic stock music and everything. The cook sighs. "Jeezis-fuggin'-cries," he says.

She lines up eight or so ketchup bottles on the bar, caps unscrewed. As she tops them off, she wonders if anyone has ever tasted the ketchup at the bottom of the bottles. "World's

---

## KETCHUP FACTS

———⊸◦◖∅◗◦⊶———

• The USDA divides ketchup into five grades based on specific gravity and total solids: Standard, Extra-Standard, Fancy, Little Lord Fauntleroy, and Umami Fist.

• Henry Heinz, a successful businessman who became unstuck in time, created his ketchup's "57 Varieties" slogan in 1896 while looking out a train window. He was inspired by a Baskin Robbins "31 Flavors" sign from 1953.

• Each American, on average, consumes 71 pounds of ketchup annually. That is the weight of three average cocker spaniels.

• Ketchup is a non-Newtonian fluid which changes its thickness and viscosity depending on how much Umami Fist is applied to it.

• "Ketchup" can alternately be spelled as *catsup*, *catchup*, or *kashyyyk*.

---

going crazy," she says, shaking her head. It's a bland thing to comment, but she's at work, and work is where she keeps her comments bland.

Duffy and Kev drag their asses out the door, each offering Maggie a weary nod.

"Drive safe, gentlemen."

The cowboy leans back from his plate. "Well, that's it," he mumbles. "We're done here," He pokes his coffee stirrer into the remains of his overcooked meatloaf. "Scuse me, ma'am?" he calls to Maggie. "Could we get three coffees to go, black?"

"You got it," she says, focused on the reketchuping.

"Make one a large with sixteen sugars please!" the little spaceman pipes in.

Maggie thinks a sec. "I'm not even sure that'll all dissolve," she calls across the empty restaurant.

The spaceman mimes unclear hand motions. "It gets wicked good when you get down to the bottom."

"Oooookay," she agrees. She caps the refilled bottles. "Two medium black, one large sugar bomb, comin' right up." The spaceman applauds her accommodation.

"Whaddaya gotta go and do that for?" the cowboy grumbles. "I told you to just take the sugar and do it yourself. We're supposed to be keepin' a low profile and you go around collecting funny looks from people."

"But the lady at the truck stop the other day got mad when I took the sugar—"

"*Packets!* You take the *packets!* Not the gaddamned glass thing offa the table!"

"Sorry, Cowboy."

The cowboy hauls himself out of the booth, making an involuntary old man groaning noise as he does so. "You're a real pain in my ass, you know that?"

Spaceman hops out of the booth. "You say that a lot."

"It's true a lot." The cowboy drops a pile of crumpled bills next to his plate. He walks stiffly over to the cash register, where Maggie is securing lids on their coffees.

"All set," she says.

"Money's on the table." He motions over his shoulder.

"Thanks very much."

The spaceman grabs the cardboard cup holder and dances around the entryway, singing a high, wavering note:

# "EEEEEEEEEEEEEEEEEEEE!!!!"

"Ignore him," the cowboy says. "He gets... excited sometimes." The rumpled man heads for the door. Spaceman tries to wave goodbye to the waitress and almost dumps the coffees.

"Couldja be goddamned careful?" Cowboy chastises.

"Jesus Nut Crunch, it's like I'm watching a four-year-old."

"Caw! Fee!" the spaceman sings in a high falsetto, to the tune of "Roxanne." He does a dead-on Sting, he thinks, and enjoys sharing his gift with others. He barrels through the door. Cowboy follows.

"Drive safe," she calls after the strangers. "Stay warm." She waves at their backs and they're gone. She clears their booth and clocks out. After a quick bathroom pit stop, she retrieves her coat and purse from the 'Kickers back room.

"Want me to wait for Beth to show up?" she asks the cook.

"Think I can handle the rush," he says, waving a finger around at the empty room without taking his eyes off the TV. She watches the news footage with him. Car fires one town over. Looks like they're blaming teenagers. "F██kin' little shits," he mumbles.

Maggie offers a non-word sound of agreement. "You on 'til 10 or 12?" She's just trying to avoid going out in the cold.

"Twelve."

"Long shift," she says. The cook nods. "Fella had big guns on him, huh?" she asks, tilting her head towards the door.

"Yup. Big calibers," the cook agrees, waiting for her to stop interrupting the TV.

"Ever shoot a gun before?"

He makes a sound that could mean fifteen different things.

Maggie nods. "Well. I'm taking off," she confirms.

"Okey-doke."

"Bye, now."

He never sees Maggie again.

MONEY'S ON THE TABLE

# BIG SNOW

EXCLUDING THE LITTLE PUFFS of frozen mist suspended in front of her mouth, the sky is clear and blue. Maggie takes a gulp of morning air and decides it might turn out to be an alright day. Duffy and Kev have favored her Ford Contour with a decent plow job. The driver's side door is frozen shut, but she's able to pop the trunk and retrieve her scraper. She chips half-heartedly at the stubborn sheet of ice coating her windshield. On the highway side of the 'Kickers lot, the two weird guys attempt to free their RENT AMERICA! moving van from its less fortunately plowed space. The cowboy heaves snow out of the way with a small brass fireplace shovel while the spaceman peers out over the too-high steering wheel. The little guy somehow reaches the gas pedal, and celebrates with stompy insistence. The van's back wheels spin uselessly, dousing the cowboy with a torrent of slush.

With the groan of cracking ice, Maggie wrenches the Contour's door open. She decides to crank the defroster on high and go back inside for ten or twenty minutes. Maybe have a hot chocolate or something. This ice scraping malarkey is for the birds. She turns the key.

THE SPACEMAN'S top-secret experimental Multi-Environment Containment Housing (Version Nine) has—an internally-powered heating unit and fluid recirculator embedded in the skin of the suit. The semi-reflective outer shell of the suit (A), along with being waterproof and pressurized for space travel, also captures solar rays and converts them into energy, which is stored in battery cells. The primary cells are located in his utility belt (B). Secondary power storage is located in the upper quarter of the helmet (C). Outside air is brought into the suit environment via a complex system of purifiers, filters and conditioning units. The Main Propulsion Cluster (MPC) located in the backpack enclosure has a thrust capability of 70,000 pounds (horizontal) and 50,000 pounds (vertical). The heads-up display (HUD, beta version 9.013n) integrated into the visor includes over one hundred view modes*. The Keypad Manipulation Controller (located on the back of the right glove) and the Voice Command Input act as the main user interfaces for all onboard systems. The spaceman has no idea how most of this hardware operates. He has been known to randomly enter number combinations into the KMC just to see what might happen. He seems constantly surprised and amazed at the random features he discovers in his MECH 9 suit.

"Hey! Check it out!" calls the spaceman, waving a fistful of wire (D) out the van window.

The cowboy spits out a mouthful of slush. "Hell's that?"

"It's like, a wicked long piece of rope?" says the spaceman. He hops out of the cab. "Look. It's on a vacuum cleaner-y reel-y thing on my belt." He shows the cowboy where the wire goes to prove he's not kidding around.

"Well, unless you're gonna pull the van outta this snowbank with your belly-button, I don't think I give a yankee doodle rolling doughnut flying f■■k-all."

After careful consideration, the spaceman says, "No, I

# MULTI-ENVIRONMENT CONTAINMENT HOUSING
### *(Version Nine)*

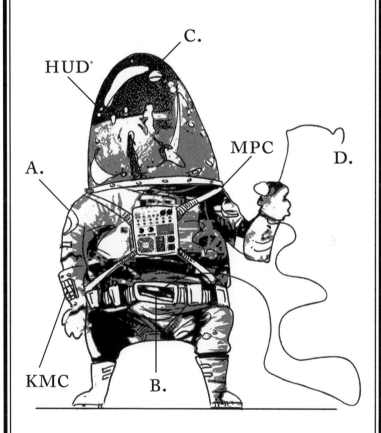

* HUD view modes include heat sensor, night vision, vector wireframe, "Money For Nothing" 3D render, and a particularly useless feature allowing the suit wearer to view their surroundings through a sepia-toned "old-timey movie reel" filter, replete with piano accompaniment.

don't think that'd work."

"Oh, no?"

"Maybe we could hook it up to the gas pedal and both push from the back. I could like, work the pedal. With the wire. I could pull the wire."

"You gotta push the pedal, not pull it," the cowboy groans, rubbing his face.

"Maybe we could build a fulcrum. A fulcrum pivot?"

"Hi, there," the waitress calls to them. She has crossed the parking lot and is standing close. The cowboy cusses himself out for not sensing her approach. He's convinced the spaceman is making him dumber.

"Uh, howdy, ma'am."

"A *pulley!* I meant a pulley," the spaceman corrects himself. "Hi!" he waves to the waitress. The cowboy wonders if the spaceman remembers who she is. He's a funny one sometimes.

"Trouble, ma'am?" The cowboy points at the Contour across the lot.

"Yeah," she admits. "Car's dead. It tends to crap out in cold weather. I wondered if I helped you get your van unstuck, maybe you could give me a lift home." She points west. "I live up the road just a bit."

"Yeah! Sure! Great!" crows the spaceman. He steps forward and shakes her hand. "What do you know about pulleys?" he asks gravely, proffering her the loose handful of wire.

"Christ on crutches," the cowboy mutters.

"I thought," she says in a kind tone, accepting the wire. "Maybe I could steer while you guys pushed."

The spaceman looks at the cowboy and points to the waitress. "Awww! That's an even better idea than the pulley!" he gushes. He presses a button on his buckle and the wire whips out of her hands and retracts back into the utility belt. He marches confidently towards the back of the van. "C'mon, Cowboy! A coupla Push Kings! That's us! You an' me! Like a coupla Clyde-Dales!"

The waitress and the cowboy stare at each other. "I mean, if it's okay with you," she says.

He chews on his chapped lower lip. "Nah, nah," and after a pause: "It's fine." He scratches the back of his neck. "Ahh," he begins. Parking lot slush drips from the brim of his hat.

"Yes?"

"We, uhh. We weren't going to use a goddamned pulley on anything. He gets these 'ideas' sometimes..." The cowboy trails off, wagging a finger at his head, assuming he's made himself clear.

She nods, smiling. "Sure."

"Right, then."

He slips and falls flat on his ass.

THE RENT AMERICA! VAN careens down the freshly-plowed road. Thanks, Duffy. Thanks, Kev.

"Where are you guys headed?" Maggie asks, tucked between them on the wide bench seat.

The cowboy raises a finger off the steering wheel and points towards the windshield.

She nods. "Uh, where are you coming from?"

He points a thumb over his shoulder.

She tries a different tack. "My name's Maggie, by the way."

"I'm Spaceman!" Spaceman chirps. He shakes her hand vigorously. The cowboy says nothing.

"Wow. A spaceman, huh. What's space like?"

The little man shrugs and draws a dog on the foggy passenger window with his finger. She motions towards the to-go tray perched on the dashboard. "You two ordered three coffees," she says to the cowboy.

Silence.

"You guys!" Spaceman whispers. "I just farted in my spacesuit *and no one can smell it but me!*"

NOT ANOTHER WORD IS UTTERED

# WINTER OF FIRE

MAGGIE LIVES IN ASPIRATIONAL HEIGHTS trailer park, Unit #14 on the end of Access Road #3. She and her cat co-exist in a two-room trailer. There is aluminum siding and flowerbeds and a mailbox, but despite the trappings of house-ness, it is not a house. She keeps it neat and doesn't socialize much with the neighbors, unless she's doing a favor for one of the old folks. They like her because she's friendly and pretty and kind to them. She doesn't have a husband or a boyfriend or a girlfriend or any friends at all, really. Just co-workers,

customers, and neighbors. No one can quite figure out why she lives here or why she's a waitress (the answers are: She's cheap, and her friend Beth got her the job).

"Well, thanks for the ride, guys," she says as they pull up to her place.

The cowboy says "Yup" while he assesses how to turn the van around.

"We're gonna miss you!" cries Spaceman, hugging her in the unselfconscious way of the young and the mentally challenged.

"Uh, yeah. Well, I'm going to miss you, too. It's been a great..." She checks her watch. "...Uh, eleven minutes."

"Yeah!" Spaceman agrees as she slides out of the van. Cowboy executes a muddy three-point turn and drives away. Walking from her mailbox to her front door, Maggie listens to the snow crunch beneath her boots.

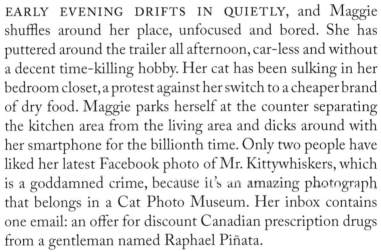

EARLY EVENING DRIFTS IN QUIETLY, and Maggie shuffles around her place, unfocused and bored. She has puttered around the trailer all afternoon, car-less and without a decent time-killing hobby. Her cat has been sulking in her bedroom closet, a protest against her switch to a cheaper brand of dry food. Maggie parks herself at the counter separating the kitchen area from the living area and dicks around with her smartphone for the billionth time. Only two people have liked her latest Facebook photo of Mr. Kittywhiskers, which is a goddamned crime, because it's an amazing photograph that belongs in a Cat Photo Museum. Her inbox contains one email: an offer for discount Canadian prescription drugs from a gentleman named Raphael Piñata.

Maggie throws her phone at a couch pillow and resolves to clean the kitchen. She opens the fridge and curses her instinct to refill the ketchup bottle. She shuffles a few condiments around. This is not how young Maggie imagined adulthood would look. There is a knock at the door.

"Who *iiiiiiiiiiis* it?" she sings in a silly falsetto, assuming it's her neighbor Mrs. Larkin, the only person who ever knocks on her door.

"Firemen, ma'am," answers a deep and serious voice.

She pauses mid-stride, only to hasten her pace to the door. "Err..." she asks as she approaches. "Is there a fire?"

"No ma'am. No, not at this juncture," the voice at her threshold answers.

Maggie peeks out her front window at the large ladder truck idling down the road. It seems a bit old to Maggie. Or a bit *something*. Firemen head towards her neighbors' trailers. *Cripes, how many of them are there?* An image of an overcrowded clown car crosses her mind. She squints through the curtains and studies the two men at her door. Their faces are obscured by mismatched helmets and oxygen masks. Maggie notes their coats and boots don't match, either, nor does their gear seem to fit particularly well. They look like trick-or-treating scarecrows She scans as much of the sky as her curtain-peeking allows. She sees no smoke. She sees no flames.

"So, uh... what can I help you with?" she asks through the door. She looks down and realizes she's holding a jar of organic pickles from the fridge. "I'm, uh... busy."

"The Department is doing a routine sweep, asking occupants to vacate their premises," the other fireman recites. "If you could please open your domicile's primary entrance, we will proceed to test its flammability and eliminate the inhabitants therein."

"What the hell?" the first fireman grumbles.

The other fireman cries: "AHHH! QUIT IT!"

Maggie knows from her youth spent on a Catholic school playground that she has just earwitnessed a wicked hard arm punch. She backs towards the kitchen, raising the pickle jar in front of her like a briny talisman. She eyes her cheap deadbolt, which is attached to her cheap door, which is attached to her cheap wall. Her home suddenly feels less like a safe space and more like a broken promise.

"Uhhhh... this is a hilarious prank, I'm sure," she says cautiously. "But you guys know you're supposed to put *out* fires and *save* people's lives, right?"

"Oh, no, ma'am. You're confusing us with firefighters," the fireman explains through the door. "They put out fires and save people."

"They're America's Heroes," the other chimes in.

"Yeah. We're firemen. We're here to burn and kill."

"People confuse us all the time. Ha-ha."

Maggie's eyes grow wide. "Cripes, it's been a weird day." A fire ax blade splits her door in two, and she screams.

———◦○◦———

THE AIR IS FILLED with smoke and the sounds of trailer park panic. Maggie hides behind her couch and tries to calm herself. She listens to distant screaming and the crackling sound of fire and acknowledges that outside, terrible things are happening to her neighbors. Mrs. Larkin. Mr. Foxx in 18. The lady with the blue hair in the blue trailer. The little prick with the BMX bike. She squeezes her eyes shut, acknowledging that she's in some deep doo herself. She clutches her jar of pickles for reassurance.

"Hell-ooooo?" a voice sings in the semi-darkness. She peers between the couch and the end table and sees the two firemen standing where her door used to be. Their names are Hal and Lenny.

"You see her?" asks Hal, peering into the dimly-lit trailer.

"Nah," says Lenny. He pokes at a splinter of door still clinging to a hinge.

Hal steps into the room. "Ehhh. Hello?" he calls. He touches the back of her recliner with his gloved hand, and smoke rises from inside the cushion. Maggie has no goddamned idea what's going on, but this is clearly not the place to be. Better to take her chances outside. *Save a neighbor? Steal a car? Call the cops? Hide in the woods?* With her heart in her throat, she swings around the end table and

WE'RE HERE TO BURN AND KILL

makes a break for it, wishing she could remember *Red Dawn*\* more clearly. In this — her time of need — she feels she could greatly benefit from a few choice nuggets of Patrick Swayze Survival Wisdom. In the end, it doesn't matter: she only gets about two steps before they grab her.

"Sorry, pretty lady," Hal says cheerfully. He picks up a magazine off the kitchen counter and it bursts into flames. He flips it over his shoulder. Her curtains ignite immediately.

"F██k!" Maggie seethes, a mixture of fear and anger. She wants to ask questions, to understand what these sons of bitches are doing. She struggles, but Lenny has her arms pinned behind her back. Heat radiates through his gloves as he squeezes tighter. Hal, though wearing a gas mask, somehow seems to smile.

"Stay calm," he says helpfully. "Everything's going to be 'okay.'" He makes the 'quote-unquote' motion with his fingers as he raises his ax high. This is when Maggie decides to kick Hal in the face.

"BAUFF!!!" he blurts, flying backwards. Lenny hits the edge of the kitchen island hard. Maggie elbows him in the ribs and he doubles over in pain. She spins free and launches the pickle jar at Hal's head. When it hits, she hears a dry, crunchy sound and his head pops right off. *Right off!* It's an economy-size jar of pickles, sure, but this still strikes Maggie as being somewhat out of the ordinary.

"The hell?" Maggie asks no one in particular. She turns back to Lenny. "What the hell?" she asks him, pointing at Hal's headless body, which is still standing by the front door. Black gooey crap squirts out of the neck stump.

"Awww, man! You killed Hal!" Lenny moans as he rubs his ribs. Hal's body catches up with the situation and flops over.

---

\* *Red Dawn* was the first movie released with a PG-13 rating. For some reason I always thought it was *Dreamscape*, and when I looked it up on The Internet, I discovered I was absolutely incorrect.

The black gooey crap, Maggie notes, gets all over the carpet. Time to skedaddle. She takes a step towards the door and sees three more firemen approaching the trailer.

"What's taking you guys so long?" one calls out.

"Let's burn burn burn," says another.

"Move it, turdherders," barks the third. He snaps his gloved fingers in a hurry-up motion.

Maggie realizes she's trapped, and is fairly certain she can't un-trap herself. Lenny picks up Hal's ax and moves towards her. The three firemen crowd the doorway. She watches the flames move from the curtains to her bookshelf. The situation seems generally negative.

Then Maggie hears yelling outside.

Then Maggie hears gunshots.

<hr />

## CRAZY ALICE

Crazy Alice is a poorly-built firearm more likely to hit a little bit of everything than a lot of something specific. Remember that scene in *The Good, The Bad And The Ugly** where Tuco assembles a reliable revolver by picking and choosing parts from a selection of guns? This is the gun the shopkeeper built out of his rejected parts. In a few pages, Cowboy will lose this old Colt forever, and he won't care because it doesn't mean all that much to him. I feel the same way about my toaster oven and my Hulu account.

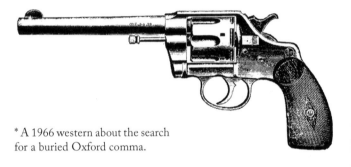

\* A 1966 western about the search for a buried Oxford comma.

BEFORE THE FIRST BODY HITS THE GROUND, Cowboy is through the doorway. In one fluid movement, he rolls over the recently punctured body of one fireman and swivels back to put a bullet into the face mask of a second. The report of his big revolver reverberates through the smoke-filled trailer. Dropping himself into the midst of the enemy, he spins on his heel, grabs Maggie by the arm, and propels them both past Lenny, whose swinging ax catches nothing but smoke. Cowboy throws himself over the kitchen counter and drags Maggie after him. They hit the peel-n-stick linoleum tiles hard.

"Stay down!" the cowboy commands. Maggie flattens herself against her cabinet doors, eyes wide, the big gun sounds still in her ears.

"Who the heck was that?" asks the fireman still standing in the doorway. The two bodies flanking him crumple to the floor — one with a hole in the front, one with a hole in the back.

Lenny begins to say: "He was like, a cowboy dude or—" but before he can finish, the very same cowboy dude inserts a bullet into the back of Len's helmet. He lets out a confused "glurk" and falls over dead, too. The remaining member of the Department decides it's in his best interest to run like hell, so he does.

"You awlright?" Cowboy asks Maggie.

"What are you doing here?"

"Passed a fire truck on the highway. Gut feeling. Knew these bastards were up to no good. They're like wet dogs at a parlor social."

"They—" she begins. "I—" She peeks over the counter top. Out the front window, she sees Mrs. Larkin's trailer engulfed in flames. "I knocked one of their heads off with a jar of pickles," she whispers.

"Yeah. Demons are like that. They're sorta brittle."

*What?* "What?" she asks. *What did he say?* "What did you say?" Near her front door, only black ooze and empty firefighting gear remain. The firemen's bodies have disappeared. Like, poof. *Ta-DA!*

"What the hell is this?" she demands. They flinch at the sound of gunfire. "And what the shit is a parlor social?"

"Just put these fires out and sit tight," he reassures her, hunkering down near her front window. "We've got a plan."

"We?" Maggie asks, remembering the little spaceman. She grabs the smoking chair cushion and douses it in the kitchen sink. "He's out there? W—with them?"

"Relax. I'm covering him," the cowboy explains. "He's prolly almost done. Just hang onto something."

"Hang on?" she repeats. "What's your plan, Cowboy?"

The cowboy offers her a lopsided grin. "He's hooking

your trailer up to our van," he says, miming a hooking-up action. He is pretty sure his plan is genius. "It's the only way I reckoned we could get you outta here without getting killed."

"Wait, you can't ju—"

"Now, relax. Everything's under control. We're gonna roll out of here in just a few—"

"Cowboy, this trailer doesn't have any *wheels*," she says.

The cowboy bites his lip and stares at the floor.

---

CHAINS HASTILY ATTACHED, the spaceman jumps back into the relative safety of the van, tossing Cowboy's big revolver Old Jake onto the dashboard. He shifts 'er into gear and hits the gas. With a decisive, jarring lurch, the spaceman sets the cowboy's escape plan into motion. It concludes one second later, as Spaceman's helmet ricochets off the steering wheel. The back tires spin to a halt in Maggie's half-frozen flower bed. Spaceman suspects the plan is not going all that well.

"Son of a—" yelps the cowboy, teetering backwards as Crazy Alice flies out of his hand. Maggie tumbles forward and ends up under her coffee table. The entirety of her material wealth shifts approximately two feet to the right and smashes to the floor. The trailer's frame buckles as it slides off its cinderblock foundation. With a burst of sparks, the main power line is severed from the circuit breaker box. The trailer goes dark, except for the burning stuff, which is now burning other stuff.

"Cowboy!" Maggie barks as she tosses the coffee table aside. "Door!" He regains his footing just in time to get tackled by a fireman rushing in. Cowboy hits the floor hard, gloved hands clamped around his throat.

"Gnurg," Cowboy chokes. He's in a sour mood.

Maggie grabs a lamp and charges across the room,

# OLD JAKE

Old Jake once put a riverboat on the bottom of the Mississippi with one shot to the hull. Old Jake is the gun that gave Half-Dick Richard his nickname. Old Jake once killed a mockingbird. Old Jake killed every member of the 1990s boy band "Take 5" at a mall food court in Orlando, Florida, only to later discover it was a group of impersonators cashing in on the band's fame, which was a common occurrence at that time. One night in San Pedro, Old Jake shot a 1991 Chevy Lumina graveyard-dead. Old Jake once shot a woman doing the Sunday New York Times crossword puzzle because she kept asking if anyone knew what a "zabaglione" was. Old Jake once launched a mouse spaceship into orbit. From 1984 to 1986, Old Jake was the host of a Tuesday morning AM call-in talk radio show about consumer rights.

Old Jake was once sent into the distant future and planted in an "Old West" museum exhibit by a master thief. While attempting to steal a valuable super-diamond from the Rare Jewel Room, the master thief led security guards on a wild goose chase through the museum, ultimately turning on them in the Old West exhibit previously mentioned, wielding Old Jake. "That ancient relic can't hurt us," declared one of the guards, who had been shooting laser pistols since he was a wee lad. Old Jake obliterated the left side of his face. The remaining guards were frightened by the loud report, unaccustomed as they were to combustion-based conflict, and ran away. The master thief escaped, and the ancient Remington was later returned to its rightful era.

Old Jake once held up a cactus.

bringing it down on the back of the fireman's neck. With an extremely satisfying crunch, he folds and hits the floor. "They *are* brittle," she says, impressed by her own strength.

"Well, yeah!" the cowboy croaks in an I-told-you-so tone. He rubs his throat. "I think he ruptured my grawlix." Cowboy turns his attention to retrieving his revolver, which has been lost somewhere amongst Maggie's burning belongings. He kicks at a nearby pile of laundry. Sneaker. Can of cat food. Remote control. Pillow on fire. "Where's my goddamned gun?" he grumbles, as if her housekeeping is to blame.

Maggie reaches over her toppled refrigerator and grabs a carton off the floor. She pours almond milk on the burning couch. It is an ineffective gesture.

"SPAAACEMAAAAN!" Cowboy hollers at the wall.

"I hear you, I hear you," Spaceman mutters in the cab of the van. There are five or maybe sixteen firemen taking cover across the access road, not yet aware that the spaceman is an absolutely terrible shot. He squeezes off another round from Old Jake, taking a fist-sized chunk out of a nearby tree. He floors the accelerator again and the van stalls out. "Oh, crackers."

"Here," Cowboy calls to Maggie across the increasingly smoke-filled trailer. "If any more of those sonsabitches try and come in, jab at 'em with this." He tosses her a broom. "I gotta find the goddamned gun."

"I'm fighting them with a friggin' broom?" she asks. *What kind of rescuer is this guy? What good will a broom do against a murderous group of psychos dressed up as firemen? Did he say 'demons' before or what?* She grasps the broom handle tighter. With her trusted pickle jar gone, she decides it is her new best friend.

"Aim for their eyes," Cowboy informs her, his attention turned back to the goddamned gun search. "They hate that."

THE TWO FIREMEN CROUCH behind the bullet-ridden tree. "Think we should go charging in?" Doug asks Denny.

"Go for it, Rambo," Denny says. "I'm good here."

"The Chief is gonna get mad if we don't kill everybody. He hates it when we don't live up to our evil potential."

Denny shrugs. "I hope that little dude quits shooting at our tree soon."

Doug clucks quietly while he ponders the situation. "Awlright," he declares, coming to a decision. "Let's grab the gas cans from the truck."

"Yeah!" Denny cries. "We're firemen!"

"Yeah!" Doug agrees. "We're freakin' *firemen*....

let's just torch the place."

WITH THE TOSS OF A MATCH, Maggie's trailer is engulfed.

"Aww, man!" Spaceman gapes at the fire in the side view mirror as the firemen scuttle back to their hiding spots, giggling and high-fiving each other. He grabs Old Jake off the dash and fires a shot out the window, hitting a propane tank on a nearby grill, which explodes. "Well, *that's* not helping." He flinches at a banging sound, fearing the firemen have snuck up behind him. It's the muted sound of fists pounding on metal. Spaceman remembers three important things:

1. THE SUN HAS JUST SET.

2. THE OLD GUY THEY KEEP LOCKED IN THE BACK OF THE TRUCK POSSESSES UNSPEAKABLE POWERS.

3. THEY HAVEN'T STOPPED FOR COFFEE IN HOURS.

There is a groaning metal sound and a sudden snap, followed by the spring-loaded ruckus of the van's rear door flying open.

"Oh, sniglets!"

Maggie, crawling across
her living room floor, hears
keys jingle. She looks up,
and through the smoke she
sees a giant silhouette in her
splintered doorway. It's a...

Well, there's a seven-foot tall
vampire standing there.

SOMETHING LIKE A SMILE

THE VAMPIRE PRESENTS HIMSELF with neither Anne Rice-ish flamboyance nor *Scooby-Doo* camp. He is an old man wearing a plain black cloak. A frightening, silver-eyed, porcelain-skinned, bloodlusting, old, old, old man. His blank, pupil-less eyes look through her, beyond her, back through millennia, past civilizations. Maggie sees the powerful jaw muscles, and the bulge of incisors beneath his thin lips. *He's thirsty*, she thinks. *Shit*, she thinks. *Shit*, she thinks again. But he doesn't feed, doesn't attack, doesn't hiss, even. He stands in her shattered doorway and stares at her. The thick smoke doesn't bother him. The wall of flames at his back doesn't affect him. Cowboy crawls over to Maggie and squints up in surprise.

"You gonna give us a gaddamned hand or what?"

Vampire offers the two humans something like a smile and turns to face the firemen.

Fun Fact: *Nosferatu* is in the public domain.

MAGGIE WATCHES THE VAMPIRE DISAPPEAR into the smoke and flames.

"Hooo-leeee-sheeet!" a fireman cries. "Is that a freakin' vampire?"

"Oh, dick!" shouts another. "That dude looks hardcore!"

"What—" Maggie begins.

"Now's not a good time for questions, waitress," Cowboy says. "Stay low and head for the exit."

"But the firemen…"

"Move!"

They crawl across the living room floor, like the safety PSAs she watched on TV when she was a kid. She has always been ready to stop, drop, and roll at a moment's notice. She's also prepared to eat vegetables and fruit, to visit the Museum Of Science, and to shame R2-D2 for experimenting with cigarettes. Smoke inhalation is maybe making her loopy. There's a broom in her hand and she can't remember where it came from. Cowboy prods her forward. "The door," he says.

"Retreat!" she hears a fireman shout in the distance. The smoke clears enough for her to see across the street. Two firemen hiding behind a tree sink into the snow. At first glance it seems like it might be an illusion, but they keep on sinking: up to their knees, waists, shoulders. And then they're gone — a retreat back into the depths of Hell, or wherever. Once they're gone, it gets awfully quiet: the soothing pop and crackle of cheap junk burning, the abandoned Department truck left idling in the middle of Access Road #3. Maggie and Cowboy slide down her front steps and flop onto her muddy front yard. She sucks in the crisp night air. Did she just see firemen drop through solid ground?

"I," she says, then nothing. She's had a hell of a night. Her eyes water up, but the cowboy can't tell if it's the stress or the smoke. "My kitty!" she cries, sitting up.

> "*I'm the big buck of this lick. If any of you want to try it, come on and whet your horns.*"
> — ABRAHAM LINCOLN

"Whoa!" Cowboy says, grabbing her by a belt loop. "I saw a fuzzy blur shoot out the door during the fight. He's safer out there than in this shit-show."

Maggie looks beyond the trees crowding the Aspirational Heights property line and says a quick prayer* for Mister Kittywhiskers. Guilt and worry twists in her belly. "Kitty..." She wipes her eyes with her sleeve. "I smell like smoke," she whispers.

Cowboy tilts a nostril in her direction. He grunts. "Time to go."

She motions towards the smouldering pile of crap that used to be her home. "But," she begins. "But I live here. My laptop. My phone... my wallet..."

"It's gone. Your stuff, my gun. We gotta vamoose, Waitress."

"Maggie."

"Listen. Maggie," the cowboy sighs impatiently. "All your neighbors are dead. The whole neighborhood's burning. Those Department goons are gonna be back for you soon. Shit just officially hit your fan, awlright?" Her jaw trembles. In a rare moment of personal revelation, Cowboy catches himself being an asshole.

He places a hand on her shoulder, and in the best gentle tone his mouth can muster, he says "I'm sorry about your, uh... shitty house."

She manages to smile. "I never even liked it."

"This is one of those moments where everything changes real fast. I'm sorry for it. I really am. Your life's different starting right now." He pauses to eye the burning trailers. "You're in danger and you gotta leave this place. You ride with us for now. Okay?"

Maggie stares at her mud-caked jeans.

"Cowwwwboooooyyy," Spaceman calls, crouched next

---

* Commonly referred to as an "Amen Break."

37

to the vampire. The old man is on his knees in the mud, exhausted.

"Ah, shit." Cowboy jogs over to the old man. "Think you can get up?" he asks. The old man doesn't respond. "I got a coffee for ya in the van." The vampire stirs at the thought of caffeine. He opens is eyes. "Mmm-hmm. Thought so. Up and at 'em." He eases Vampire back to his feet.

Cowboy holds out an open palm. Spaceman returns Old Jake (butt-first as he'd been taught. Ha-ha. Butt). He mumbles about not doing so good. "You did good enough, cos we're still here." Cowboy says, giving a critical squint down the barrel. He re-holsters the revolver with a practiced double spin which — under normal circumstances — would cause Maggie to giggle and ramble about corny old spaghetti westerns. But the circumstances feel super-not-normal, and she's wondering if she's in shock or high on toxic fumes or something. Having a corny gunslinger cowboy hero-man around actually feels extremely reassuring at the moment, so she sits blankly in a puddle and says nothing.

"I think the van's busted," Spaceman says. "Those dashboard lights were blinking."

"What lights?"

"The the uh…" He paddles the air with his hand. "What do they call 'em?… Dummy lights."

The cowboy takes a deep breath. "Well, what did they *say?*"

"I don't know. They're dummy lights."

Maggie walks towards them, jeans soaked. "Is he gonna be okay?" she asks, nodding at the vampire. The old man stands as still as a statue, waiting to be led back to the van.

Cowboy fishes a wooden coffee stirrer out of his breast pocket and jams it between his teeth. "Why don't you unhook the trailer," he says to Spaceman, ignoring her question. "See if the van'll start now. I reckon you just flooded it." The spaceman gives a thumbs-up and skips off across the icy road. Maggie looks in the open bay of the RENT AMERICA!

van and catches a glimpse of half-opened moving boxes, a headboard, and mismatched furniture piled high on the sides of the cargo area. In the middle of the mess sits an ancient, battered coffin. Cowboy watches her go awful pale. He taps her on the shoulder and motions towards the vampire. They lead him by the elbows, gently guiding him back to the van. "Time to go," the cowboy says again, to no one in particular.

# MEDDLERS

HENRY DESCENDS THROUGH THE SNOW, the asphalt, the soil, the rock. For an infinite moment, the demon drops. When he reaches the Department, he lands on his head. This happens every time he gets killed. He grabs the brass pole mounted in the center of the room and pulls himself to his feet. He replaces his lost helmet and boot from the pile of spare gear in the corner and reports to the Chief's office.

He knockity-knocks on the door and enters.

"What went wrong?" The Chief is usually no-bull.

"Some crazy dudes showed up and ruined everything!"

"Elaborate."

"Welllll, we got some good flames going, y'know? Did a lotta really great killing and stuff. You woulda *loved* it, Chief! But then a hat dude and a short dude showed up and rescued this chick, and then there was a scary vampire th—"

"A vampire?"

"Yeah, Chief! Yeah! Dude was about to fang our asses!" He mimes teeth with his fingers. "It was so freaky, we got the crap outta there! Booked it like Dano!"

"God forbid you should get in a fight," the Chief says dryly.

"I know, right?"

The Chief exhales. "I don't like do-gooders interfering with my master plan of evil-spreading. I like to make bad things happen, Henry. You *know* this."

"They're a bunch of buttinskis, is what they are, Chief."

"Could you just *try* to shut up, Henry?"

"Sure, Chief."

The office is silent as the Chief contemplates. Henry shifts his weight from one foot to the other, wondering if maybe he's been dismissed. "I want the meddlers eliminated," the Chief decides. "You've got their scent, yes?" The fireman points at his gasmask and nods enthusiastically. "I want their stupid evil-fighting faces peeled off and mounted in a three-ring binder. I want it on my desk by end-of-day Friday."

The demon snaps a salute. "Right on, sir. Totally." He hotfoots it out of the office. The Chief sits on the edge of his desk, oblivious to the mess around him. He sighs.

"Meddlers," he grumbles, shaking his head.

*"People certainly have been confused
for a long time."*
—LAU TZU, TAO TE CHING (300BC)

# PART TWO

## Off Ramps & Coffee

IN WHICH OUR HEROES TRAVEL THE
HIGHWAYS AND BYWAYS OF THIS
GREAT NATION AND GET GENERALLY
ANNOYED WITH EACH OTHER.

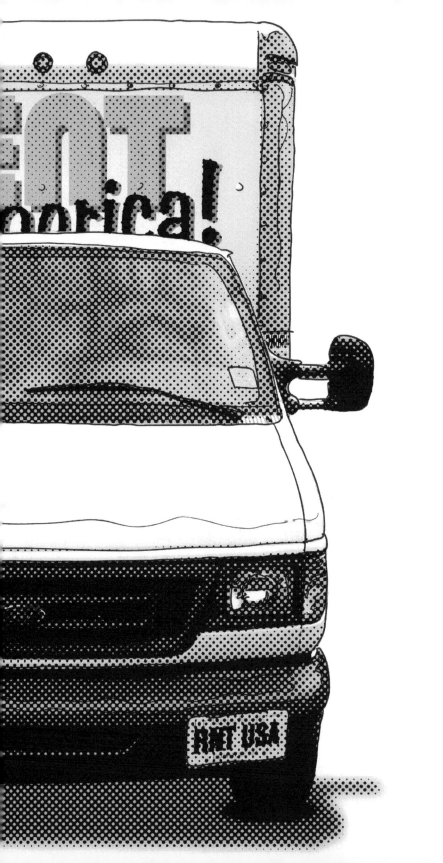

# RENT AMERICA!

THE RENT AMERICA! FLEET consists of eight hundred E-350 Ford Econoline 15-foot box vans deployed across the United States, with the exception of New Mexico, due to pending litigation which the company cannot comment on at this time. Vehicle #BR26354 has been in service since 1999 and has crossed the continent one hundred and forty-two times in an erratic pattern typical of one-way hauling. It is a unique member of the RENT AMERICA! family.

Built in the Metuchen, New Jersey Ford plant, it was originally designated as a classified Level Alpha Plus Federal Government vehicle.* It was equipped with a 6.8L efi V10, a TorqShift 5-speed automatic transmission and an extra-heavy-duty dual 260-amp electrical system. A heavy duty suspension held up a reinforced mine-proof subframe. Instead of being shipped to a top secret government agency inside a hollowed-out mountain, a clerical error at the factory caused the radar-absorbent carbonyl iron ferrite exterior to be painted white and decaled with bright, happy graphics. #BR26354 was delivered to RENT AMERICA! headquarters. Soon families, retirees, and vacationers were watching the United States' majestic vistas drift past through polycarbonate thermoplastic bulletproof glass.

On the van's final rental run, two newlyweds anticipated a busy moving day to their new house. Their fully packed RENT AMERICA! van sat in front of their apartment building while the couple slept on their empty living room's floor. When they awoke the next morning, ready to begin an exciting new phase of their relationship, the van was gone. Stolen.

---

* http://www.fleet.ford.com/programs/government/

# INVENTORY

MAGGIE WAKES UP ALONE, splayed across the RENT AMERICA! bench seat, a floral pattern comforter draped over her. The van is parked in front of a Goodsack Food Mart, the gross-orange glow of the shopping plaza's halogen lights illuminating

> "Up, sluggard, and waste not life; in the grave will be sleeping enough."
> — BENJAMIN FRANKLIN

the pile of empty coffee cups on the dashboard. She'd had a work dream, something about her and the vampire running a busy restaurant. She had burst into the kitchen, harried and impatient, telling him to hurry up already. He'd smiled, leaning over the stove, clearly not intending to hurry up already. Then her cat leaned out of the manager's office, a giant feline wearing a shirt and tie. *Table Seven is waiting!* Mr. Kittywhiskers had shouted.

Maggie rubs her eyes, smoke clogging her pores. The dash clock tells her she's only been asleep for an hour and a half — just long enough to feel exhausted. The dashboard display also tells her the temperature, their GPS location, her social security number, and a medical scan revealing a precancerous growth in her lung. It's a hell of a vehicle.

She slides across the seat and opens the passenger door. The supermarket is familiar, only a couple towns away from 'Kickers. These things feel very past tense to her. Old job, former residence, past life. She crawls out of the truck and swings the door shut. It **WHOOMPH**s like a refrigerator. Across the empty parking lot, the spaceman lays in the bottom of a shopping cart, propelling himself in big lazy circles with his MECH-9 rockets set to 2% thrust. He clatters over.

"Hi!" he chirps. "Wanna ride in it?"

"No. Not right now, Spaceman."

"Ahhhh, *cammmaaann.*" He circles slowly. "It's *funnnnnn.*"

"What are we doing here? Where's Cowboy?" Her mouth is gross and mungy. She no longer owns a toothbrush.

"Food? Maybe some coffee. COFFEE!"

She looks at the GoodSack. "I think they're closed."

The supermarket's doors swing open and Cowboy shuffles out. "Hey," he calls, crossing the lot. He hands a pamphlet to the spaceman. "I got us some work for tonight. All signed up. Pays cash. Should help us cover a few expenses."

"Expenses?" Maggie asks

"Breakfast, coffee, g—"

"COFFEE!" Spaceman shouts.

"—gas, ammo. We only got one bullet left."

"**GoodSack Night Stocking**," Spaceman reads from the pamphlet. "**Exciting work in a friendly environment.** *Oooh!* That *does* sound fun!" His tone, Maggie notes, is free of sarcasm.

"Figured you'd be out cold for the rest of the night," Cowboy points at the van. "Why dontya go lie down again? You and Vampire been through a lot tonight. Rest."

She's beat for sure, but the thought of being locked in a van with a vampire doesn't sound particularly conducive to relaxation. "I could use a diversion from thinking about..." She waves over her shoulder. "Life."

"Y'sure?"

"Yeah. I'll help you guys out," she yawns. "I mean, you saved my ass tonight. I at least owe you guys gas money."

Spaceman hugs her waist. "This is gonna be *so great!*"

"Easy," she warns.

"We got a couple hours to kill before the shift starts," the cowboy says, scratching his whiskers. "Wanna learn how to clean a gun?"

"No, I don't," she says, squinting at the closed businesses across the road. She points. "If I remember correctly, there's an old movie theater thataway."

Cowboy scratches the back of his head. "Thataway, it is."

❧

THE LOCAL MOVIE THEATER is a fine 1940's-era movie house. Not restored or remodeled or anything fancy, but clean and warm. The trio walk into the midst of an underattended all-night Akira Kurasawa marathon. Cowboy grumbles about samurai but sits down anyway. Spaceman reads the subtitles out loud while he tosses popcorn into a slot on his front control panel. Maggie slouches in her seat and tries to pick up the thread of the plot. Villagers attacked by bandits. Hero samurai. Her mind drifts to the screams and gunfire of a few hours earlier. About halfway through *Yojimbo*, the cowboy elbows her, ejecting her from a nap she didn't realize she'd been taking.

"What!" she yelps, jolting upright. There are a few disapproving exhales in the darkness.

He puts a calming hand on her knee. "You were snorin'."

"Ugh," she groans, sinking back into a slouch and rubbing her face. She blinks hard and tries to focus on the screen.

"I want you to hold onto something for me." He reaches into his shirt and pulls out a cross on a chain.

"Oh," she says, surprised. "I mean, thanks?"

"This is a vampire-related transaction."

"Sure."

"He's okay with you. I think he's taken a bit of a shine to you, actually. But Vampire's a hard one to read sometimes." Cowboy waves his hand across his face.

"Is he... dangerous?"

"He's a peach with us. No holes in my neck or anything." She tries to confirm this but the theater is too dark. Cowboy motions towards the spaceman. "I'm not even sure that one *has* a neck," he mumbles. "The old man's given up on the whole bloodsucking business, supposably."

"He has?" she asks. "They can *do* that?"

Cowboy fidgets in his seat and stares at the movie screen. "For our sakes, we'd better hope so."

"Is he going to be okay?"

"No. I reckon not."

Onscreen, Sanjuro massacres six guards. "Whoooaa, cooool!" Spaceman exclaims. He's watching *LazyTown* on his HUD.

"Where are you guys headed, Cowboy?"

"Graveyard, I suppose."

"Serious answer."

He sighs and picks at nonexistent lint on his pants. "We're helping the old man get home."

"Where's that?"

"Sorta feeling that out as we go. We're close, I think."

"And what do the firemen have to do with it?"

He shrugs. "Nothing." Sanjuro trashes a sake factory. "They're just assholes."

Maggie snorts.

"And they got your number. That smoke you smell? On your clothes an' skin? That don't wash off. You're marked."

"You, too?"

Cowboy nods. "There's no escaping them. They'll keep coming. We'll keep moving 'til we can get the vampire where he's going. After that..."

She waits. "After that what?"

"We stop running."

She clips the chain around her neck and tucks the cross into her shirt. "Thanks."

He grunts. "Don't lose it. It belonged to someone special."

"Are you guys going *steeeaaady* now?" Spaceman asks, giggling.

They both tell him to shut up.

ABOUT HALFWAY
THROUGH YOJIMBO

AS THEY TRUDGE DOWN THE AISLE towards the GoodSack back room, it occurs to Maggie she's never been in a closed supermarket before, and it's weird. She's accustomed to the familiar consumer experience of a too-bright warehouse full of people and fruit and shiny tiled floors. Big signs, cool aisles, the distant bleeps of cash registers. Kids shouting at cereal boxes, squeaky shopping cart wheels, Muzak. But this? Stillness and emptiness and dimness and silence. Shadows in a normally shadowless land.

The night manager is a middle-aged woman named Denise. Her thick-lensed glasses distort her eyes, making her look constantly bewildered. Denise gathers her crew of temps and explains how the inventorying will work*. Maggie tunes out to survey her new co-workers. She recognizes a customer from 'Kickers. Nice guy, decent tipper. His name is Mike, maybe. There's a woman whose skin is the same color as the supermarket's floor. She is christened "Floor Face." Maggie looks down the row of night shift workers: Oldest Lady Ever, Glenn Danzig, Fatty, NASCAR Bro, Total Creep, and a few others who are unnicknameable.

The temp workers are paired into two-person teams. Maggie and Spaceman get assigned to the cereal aisle. They inventory things like Quispy Qurls For Girls and Healthy Life Sugar Raisin Corn Smacks for Heart-Smart Seniors. Maggie is silent for most of the shift, contemplating her material losses and missing her cat terribly. She can't comprehend how she's supposed to show up for work tomorrow. The to-do list required to be done between now and morning seems insurmountable. Clothes? Shower? Insurance? Eating? She should probably take the day off, right?

* Move down the aisle, left to right, top to bottom, do not skip any sections unless otherwise marked. Fill in every column on the worksheets provided: Area. Department. Piece Count. Dollar Amount. UPC. Worksheet Number. Verified By. Initial the blue slip taped to the shelf.

Spaceman babbles non-stop, telling her plots to movies she's never heard of and television shows he's never seen. He describes his old space station and the things his spacesuit can do. He tells her about his childhood, which is actually a plot from an old ABC After School Special.

"Spaceman," she finally interrupts. "Why are you here?"

"The lady told me to count these!" he cries defensively, shaking cereal boxes in the air.

"No, I mean, in the van. On this trip."

"I'm helping Cowboy help the old guy."

She marks down a box of Fruity Bits. "But *why?*"

"The cowboy and me are bestest friends! Best pals ever!"

"You guys don't seem..." She bites her lip. "Cowboy seems like he needs a break from you sometimes."

"Aww, he's an ol' grumpydump! He's my oldest bestest friend in the whole woooorld." He picks up a pricegun and stickers his arm.

"How long have you known him?"

The MECH-9 suit dearchives the video clip of Spaceman meeting Cowboy and plays it on his heads-up display: Spaceman waits in the RENT AMERICA! van, parked on the shoulder of a stretch of desert highway. The cowboy crests a dune, sunburnt, windburnt, soulburnt. He drags a coffin by a chain. Spaceman reads the clip's metadata.

"Three months, fourteen days, seven hours."

Maggie nods. "That's your longest friendship?"

He bobs his head.

"What's gonna happen after you get Vampire home?"

He tears open a box of SugarFist BlamBalls. "Awww, no way! A decoder ring!" The spaceman, wearing a two billion dollar spacesuit that can perform 39.44 petaFLOP/s*, is mightly impressed by the plastic toy. He frees it from its wrapper. "*Sssssooo rrrrraaaad!*"

It breaks.

> \* That's almost forty thousand million million flops.

---

Cowboy is assigned the Health & Beauty endcaps, teamed with The Oldest Lady Ever, who might be upwards of one hundred and fifty years old. Her deathly slow pace is almost unfathomable. *How can a human body move this slowly without ceasing to live?* Cowboy pushes his rage down. He's very good at it. They count soap, body wash, shampoo, conditioner. He counts her sections for her. "Just initial the slips. Initial them. Just." He intitials her slips for her, too.

---

## ZESDT

ZESDT synthetic detergent soap-like bath bars come in a variety of scents, including Aqua Aloe Pure Burst, Ocean Spring Seaman's Delight, Clean Lint, Ultimate Freshness Energy Explosion (with Stimulating Wetness Effects), Bill Pullman, Arcane Incantation, Tropical Fish Mist, and Tub Dumper.

THE INVENTORY CREW gathers in the GoodSack's windowless break room. They sit in silence with brown-bagged sandwiches and yogurt cups, listening to earbuds and playing with their phones. The only sound in the room besides the buzzing fluorescent light is Spaceman slapping the tabletop and singing an Elvis Costello song. He doesn't know any lyrics, but he's quite content howling nonsensical mouth sounds.* Maggie drinks what many would call coffee. "Why didn't we bring snacks?" she moans.

Cowboy grunts, pushing the Spaceman one chair over so he can have his back to the wall.

Mike Maybe tosses a pack of Twazzlers onto the table. "Go crazy. My treat."

"AWWWWWESOMMMMMME!" cheers the spaceman, tearing open the package. He extracts two red Twazzles and inserts them into his control panel. There is a click and a whir. He giggles weirdly.

"Much appreciated," The cowboy nods, tipping his hat but not indulging. He leans back in his chair and considers trying to catch a quick mid-shift siesta.

"Yeah, thanks," Maggie agrees, pulling off a strip of red chewable material. Under normal circumstances, she'd never eat crap like this, but the gesture is kind and she's hungry. She jaws on it like a son of a bitch.

"I know you," Mike Maybe says to her, squinting an eye and pointing. "You work at 'Kickers, yeah?"

"Yah," she answers in a funny, glued-teeth voice. "Gdickerz," she nods and smiles.

"I saw the news report about that crazy business up the way yesterday. The fires." His voice darkens a tone.

Maggie chews slower. "Yah. Crajy."

"The fuggin' black kids drove up from the city," pipes in

---

* _Wella usa beesa bing bang, nowa daisy-dukey doo! Buh thenna wig a ibba bunted, an now I sawba wabba bing you say!_

Total Creep. The man is hunched over a counter covered in pamphlets about teamwork and proper lifting techniques, chewing on a cold meatball sub and playing a game on his phone. "Everyone's dead. Fuggin' gangs, y'know."

"Whab?" Maggie responds, incredulous of the racist bullshit pouring out of the man's gross mouth. Mike Maybe concentrates on his sandwich.

"I seen it on the teevee," the Creep says. "Friggin' gang initiation. They drove up there last night in their friggin' pimpmobiles and friggin' lit a bunch of fuggin' people on fire."

> ## PATENTS FOR MACHINES THAT MAKE PAPER BAGS
>
> ⚬⚬⚬⚬
>
> US PATENT NO. 9,355
> US PATENT NO. 12982
> US PATENT NO. 20,838
> US PATENT NO. 123,811
>
> Source. *Small Things Considered* by Henry Petroski (2003, Knopf)

"Whab? Thab didn't habben!" she garbles out. Cowboy places his hand on Maggie's knee. "Whab?" She turns to him and tries swallowing for the tenth time. "You know that's not what happened!"

Total Creep smiles at the floor. His crooked teeth trap flecks of shredded iceberg lettuce. "It was on the teevee. Teevee don't lie. The cops picked up a carload of 'em on the innerstate. The friggin' jig-a-booze—"

"F█K THIS!" Maggie leaps to her feet, her folding chair clattering back. "I—" She is too angry to articulate anything. "Thanks for the snack," she mutters to Mike. She tries to communicate her rage by slamming the door on the way out. The hissing hydraulic mechanism cheats her of the satisfaction.

The room falls silent, except for the occasional crinkle of a fast food wrapper. In the corner, Floor Face picks at the edge of a large display sign shoved behind stacks of paper bags.

# MOUNTAINS OF
## FLOWERS AND FRUIT!

it proclaims. The cowboy parks his worn-out boot heels on the table and tips his hat over his eyes. The spaceman takes two more red licorice strips and inserts them into his gastro unit. The Creep is emboldened to continue.

"The friggin' ni—"

"You'd be wise to shut it, friend," the cowboy warns from under his hat. He rests his hand on the butt of his holstered Remington. The Creep eyes the iron. "Shut it good and tight."

---

THE SUPERMARKET LOADING DOCK IS STILL. The moon hangs in the blackness like a single clear peg on a Lite Brite sky, reflecting off the blank expanse of concrete wall. Maggie slouches by the fire exit, smoking a cigarette she bummed off Glenn Danzig.

*"One brave deed makes no hero."*
— JOHN GREENLEAF WHITTIER

"Motherf■■ker," she mutters. She wants to punch something because she's angry, but she's not angry enough to intentionally hurt her hand. Her practicality makes her angrier, but still not enough to punch anything (which infuriates her). She wants to kick the Creep in the nuts. Hard. Really put 'em up the back of his throat.

The heavy emergency exit door opens and Cowboy joins her. Maggie kicks at some dirty snow. "Why didn't you say anything?" she asks.

He wants a drag of her cigarette real bad, but opts to chew

on another coffee stirrer. "Now, listen. If I say it's not his fault, I don't want you to m—"

"*Are you kidding me?*"

"—misunderstand. He's a right asshole, for sure. What I'm tryin' to get at is the Department. The Firemen. They're Evil. Capital E Evil, comprendé?" Maggie scowls. "They don't just burn shit, they sow seeds of distrust, fear, terror. They manipulate the weak-minded." He taps his temple with the coffee stirrer.

Maggie nods again. "Okay. So assholes are completely blameless. Check. Roger wilco."

Cowboy grimaces and waves his hands. "That asshole in there, he's an ignorant shit, I ain't contestin' that. Our job—" He stands straighter. "The people who fight Evil, the Heroes — Our job is to protect shitheads like him. Protect 'em and pity 'em."

"This is some kind of good versus evil thing for you?"

He nods. "We're the good ones." She snorts. "What's so damned funny?"

"It's sort of simplistic, don't you think? You sound like you got your moral code from a comic book."

"You gotta fight for something. What do you fight for?"

She takes a drag, closing one eye to the smoke. Off the top of her head, she can't think of anything she's ever fought for. She's sure there's something. It'll come to her. She shrugs. "I'm just living my life."

Cowboy twists the coffee stirrer between his teeth. "Well, that got you this far. Hope you got a Plan B."

Maggie stares at the ground. Cowboy slumps against the wall. "I—" he begins. "Listen, I'm no good at explaining stuff. What the shit do I know. You've had a helluva night. Lost a lot of neighbors. I didn't come out here to..." He sighs. "You're in shock. You've got the, uh..." He twirls a finger. "Survivor's guilt."

"What do you know about survivor's guilt?"

He bites down on the coffee stirrer. "I dunno."

She gives him a sarcastic thumbs up.

"Maybe you oughta screw this gig and take the rest of the night off, huh?" he suggests.

"I don't quit."

"Well, maybe you should."

She closes her eyes. Fire. Screams. A row of ketchup bottles. "I've got nothing to go back to."

"Welcome to the club."

They hear giggling from behind the steel door. The cowboy cracks it open in time to see Spaceman cruising past on an electric handtruck. "EEEEEEE!!!" the little man squeals, swinging a portable price scanner around like a pistol. "PEE-YOW!" he cries, shooting Cowboy squarely in the eyes. He hollers a goddamnit. The spaceman veers around a pallet of potato chips and disappears down the hall as the door swings shut.

"JESUS-CHRISTMAS-ON-A-CANDY-CANE-CROSS!" Cowboy exclaims, jamming his palms into his eye sockets. He blinks at red blobs dancing around the loading dock. "Bastard!" Maggie stares at the shadows beyond the parking lot and says nothing.

"I gotta go catch up with that space turd." Cowboy says. "He's off on one of his sugar fits again." He looks up at the moon and reckons they've got about five minutes of break time left and tells her so. He heaves the door open and goes space turd searching. Following the trail of knocked-over boxes, Cowboy tries to massage the red spots from his vision. He'll never aim true again.

—⋅◦⊂⊛⊃◦⋅—

TWO HOURS BEFORE OPEN, THE GOODSACK FOOD MART is restocked and ready to serve its customers. Out in the parking lot, the sun offers little warmth to the night shift crew shuffling towards their cars. Maggie, Spaceman, and Cowboy huddle by the RENT AMERICA! van. Total Creep skulks near the newspaper boxes, staring at his phone.

"Whelp," says the cowboy. "That was a night." The spaceman hands him his earnings for the evening, a small pile of bills. The cowboy nods.

"Oh, right," Maggie says, embarrassed. Her money had gone from Denise's palm right into her damp jeans pocket. She digs it out as a road salt-covered Chevy Cavalier rolls up in front of them. The window cranks down and there's Mike Maybe's red cheeks.

"Hey, gang," he says cheerfully, addressing Maggie. "I've got a day job up north and was going to hit 'Kickers for one of those Breakfast Burrito Blasts. Was wondering if you needed a ride to work."

"Oh," she says, startled. Is this where she goes back to waiting tables? Is she supposed to put on a smile and go buy new pots and pans? Check Craigslist for an apartment? Oh God, is she supposed to go talk to the police? The *police?* She looks to her new friends but their eyes are elsewhere: Cowboy pokes at nothing with the toe of his boot while Spaceman watches infomercials on his heads-up display. "Oh," she says again.

"I mean," Mike backtracks. "I'm not, uh, hitting on you or anything. My wife wouldn't approve of that sort of business." Ha-ha.

"No, no!" Maggie says. "No, I didn't think that." Total Creep leans against a support column and stares at her. She thinks about the line cooks and the waitresses and the customers at 'Kickers. She doesn't feel anything. Not a damned thing.

"Um, thanks very much for the offer, but me and m…

my brothers here..." — she motions to the cowboy and the spaceman, who are still pretending to not be listening — "We're heading west." She points out past the Pine Plaza sign, which is actually south. Doesn't really matter. "Visiting our, uh, grandparents."

"Oh. All right," Mike nods with a smile. "Well, have a good time." A part of him is relieved to not have a long car ride with her. He likes pretty girls just fine, but they're unnerving creatures.

"If anyone asks," she adds. "Don't mention you saw me, okay?"

"Sure, sure." He salutes and rolls up his window. Maggie hears the parking brake release and the Chevy rolls out of her life. She turns to the cowboy and holds out her small offering of money.

"Grandparents, huh?" he grins. It's a pretty good smile, she thinks.

"Vampire reminds me of my Gramp a little," she shrugs. "In an undead sort of way."

"We're a team now!" the spaceman announces, grabbing her hand. "A super hero team," he says solemnly. She withdraws her hand and pats his helmet.

The cowboy crams the wad of bills into his pocket and scans the horizon. "I think I saw a **DUNK-A-DONUT** up the road. Coffee."

"COFFFFEEEEEE!!!" Spaceman cries, raising his arms in victory. The gesture triggers something in the MECH-9's programming, launching him about two hundred feet in the air. His rocket pack lowers him gently back to the asphalt. "That was weird huh."

Maggie and Cowboy stare at him, hair blown back, snow and road salt and gum wrappers stuck to their faces.

"Coffee," he says in a tiny voice.

∞•◦≫∘⬦∘≪◦•∞

# THE BLACK VAN

"DID YOU COPY that blip, Strzempko?" asks Agent Kriger, excited but composed. He's a professional. "I need signal confirmation." He tilts his laptop screen back to see it better.

"Roger that, Kriger," Agent Strzempko winks, scanning the data scrolling down his own monitor. "It's gone cold but it was a solid read."

"Can we pinpoint it?" Agent Sluben asks.

"Negative."

"God damn it," Kriger spits, pounding his fist on the folding table. "Closing in on the little bastard, though. Sluben, ballpark a region of interest and add it to the board."

"Done," replies Sluben, He wheels his office chair across the cramped work space the three field operatives share. He glances over Strzempko's shoulder, double-checks the coordinates, and draws a circle on a map taped to the inner wall of the Space Agency's Rogue Hardware Retieval van. There are other circles on the map, connected by lines, signifying a path from nowhere to somewhere.

"Smoke break. You're in charge." Kriger says, slapping Strzempko on the back. He mashes his testicles against the adjuster knob on the back of the agent's office chair as he squeezes past him. Goddamned van. "Be ready to move as soon as we get a hot sig." He opens the van's rear door and he and Sluben step out into the damp mountain air. They put distance between themselves and the hum of cooling fans and spinning hard drives. Kriger lights a Pall Mall and takes a long drag. Beyond the guardrail, he sees trees, railroad tracks, trees, a church steeple, trees, and cell phone towers camouflaged to look like a trees. Somewhere out there is missing Space Agency property: a MECH unit, version 9.

*Six months of RHR, Jesus.* Kriger shakes his head in wonder. *Tracking, triangulating, closing in, missing something, letting it slip through their grasp, again and again. The Agency heads crying inefficiency, the lab nerds saying his team can't operate the tracking equipment properly.* He smooths his tie. *Bureaucracies,* he thinks. *Maybe if the f▪▪king tracking unit they designed into the f▪▪king suit worked right it wouldn't be so f▪▪king hard to find the f▪▪king thing. Maybe if our van wasn't such an enormous piece of defective shit we'd be able to chase the signals we get.*

"The new Disruption Beam is set up and ready," Sluben says, pointing to a multi-directional array velcroed to the roof of the black van. "Next time we get a hot signal, that suit is ours."

They walk back towards the van. "I bet *he'll* love that." The men laugh. Kriger raps on the tinted driver's side window. "Hear that, buddy? We're gonna get your pal back soon."

"Very good," the driver responds through the glass.

Sluben holds up his hand. "Can I get a high five?" They laugh again.

"Your humor continues to elude me, gentlemen."

"Don't leave me hangin'!" Sluben buckles under the weight of his un-high-fived hand. Kriger doubles over, cracking up at his colleague's mock-struggle. They've been on the road for too damned long. He's gonna lose his mind.

⸺⸺∞⧉∞⸺⸺

TIME PASSES

# CONVENIENCE

"AND THEN," THE BOY EXCLAIMS, slouching behind
the Pump-N-Zoom Express counter. "There's a gi-normous
explosion! **PHKLLEOOWW***!!*" Spit flies, causing Banjo —
his dog and sole audience member — to flinch. "'Commander
Hero swoops his hover-board across the dunes, chasing the
diabolical glue monster back to his desert lair!'" Myron pops
a powdered donut in his mouth (he will occasionally mark a
package as damaged and enjoy a free snack. This is his version
of rebellion). "He's fearless!" the boy says through dusted lips.
Banjo licks his paw in agreement. "The glue monster tries to
trap the commander against its sticky body with a deadly
embrace, but Commander Hero ducks low and socks it with
an uppercut!"

**POW***!*

"He hauls the monster to his underground jail and shouts
his catchphrase:

**HUBRIS***!*

"Haw! I love it when he says that!"

Myron Hayden craves this adventure. His meek and
clumsy existence begs for it. Heroism. Confidence. Skill. He
knows he has a fantastic name, a name of great destiny. He
awaits the moment when he can boldly step forward and save
the day, to say his name to a bad guy in a cool, gravelly voice.
On that day he shall cast off his Pump-n-Zoom Express
apron, he will toss aside his glasses as his vision magically
sharpens, and he will Do What Needs To Be Done. Maybe
his acne will clear up, too. And hopefully there will be girls
around to notice. Like, smokin' hot girls.

An electronic chime lets him know a sedan has just pulled
up to pump four. He glances out the window. He doesn't
need to do anything but sit there. That's his job.

FFFZZZZZZZZZZZZZZZZZZZZZZZZZZZZZ

THINK YOU SHOULD CHECK THE FUEL INJECTOR YOU NEED TO REMOVE THE AIR IN

CALLER SEVEN!
OU'VE WON TICKETS TO SEE

MICKEY DOLE

IN PIPPEN

go into the cluuuuh
listen to the duuubbb,
ive a little ruuuub, to that azz in tha-

COLLEGE COLONIAL THE.

FFZZZZZZZZZZZZZZZZZTT

the political front, today it v

-ainst my heart, that was the haaaaro

iitationsapply.nowseedealerfordetailsofferexpires

That's the differe

between hip-hop

cultural moveme

hip-hop as a cons

nced that
the long
ed States,
mpion of -

- WE'RE BACK IT'S ME YOUR MAIN MAN J-R

COMIN' AT YA ON THE ROCKINEST sta

THAT REALLY ROC

SUNDAY! SUNDAY! AT T

FLEET STAPL

TWEETER CENTER

ND WE'VE GOT HIM IIIILLLLZZZZZZZZZ

N THE LINE NOW!

ELLO? MR. FORTIN

...they're not *illegal* immigrants, th
*immigrants.* You understand that t

"WILL YOU STOP PLAYING with the goddamned scan button on that thing?"

"But I was just—"

"Just just! Just pick a friggin' station!"

"Oh, Cowboy, give him a break. He—"

"Listen, I don't—"

"Now calm dow—"

"Don't tell me to calm—"

"I gotta pee."

The RENT AMERICA! van careens down the highway, winding its way out of the snowy mountains while the heater pushes out an inadequate warmth. Maggie sticks her numb hands into the dashboard vents, her fingertips brushing against a dense blockage of jellybeans and parking lot receipts and pennies and pen caps.

"Spaceman's gotta pee," she says.

"I heard him. Do you think I didn't hear him?"

"Well, you didn't respond."

"I don't need to respond. I'm driving. I'm concentrating on the goddamned road. Do you want us to go off a cliff or something?"

"We're not going off any cliffs. There are no cliffs. We've been driving for seven damned hours straight. Are we going to pull over soon or what?"

"I just peed in my suit," the spaceman states. "I don't need to pee anymore."

"Ewww!! You just peed in your suit? That's gross!"

"I'm warm. Suit runs on pee."

"Gorramned loon," Cowboy mumbles.

"I could hook my suit up to the heater vent..." Spaceman reaches for his utility belt.

"NO!" the cowboy and the waitress shout.

"You'll break something," says the cowboy.

"I don't want your pee-air in my face," says Maggie.

The spaceman shrugs. "Fine. Whatever." He turns a dial

on his suit's chest panel. Warm.

They drive in silence. They pass a cop car and a pulled-over Saab. The officer stands in the breakdown lane, facing the driver. Drunk driving? Drug bust? They drive by too fast to ever know.

"Coffee!" Spaceman shouts at the ceiling.

"Coffee," Maggie nods. "Sure, let's get some coffee." The spaceman hops up and down in his seat. Cowboy stews. Maggie points at an upcoming sign. "Gas station ahead."

## HORIZONTAL GAZE NYSTAGMUS TEST

A police officer holds a pen fifteen inches from the bridge of a suspected drunk driver's nose. The officer moves the pen to the left and right, checking for smooth eye movement (i.e. Smooth Pursuit), and steady eyes when looking at the extreme right or left (Distinct Nystagmus At Maximum Deviation). The officer estimates the angle at which the eye twitches; if twitching occurs at less than 45 degrees, it is a sign of inebriation. The test has been proven to be effective only when conducted with PaperMate pens. The use of Bic pens has led to hundreds of needless deaths every year.

THE RENTAL VAN pulls up to the pump island. Cowboy puts 'er in Park, cussing the road and the sky and the world for no particular reason. Maggie attempts to tidy the cab of the van, dumping a cup of deceased dashboard coffee onto the concrete. She extracts a GoodSack bag from the depths of the bench seat and begins gathering crap.

**COLA!** shouts a sign next to the van. **6 PKS 1.99+DEP.**
Spaceman reaches for a can from the large display of six-packs next to the gas pump, only to discover it's an illusion, a cardboard box pretending to be a large display of six-packs next to a gas pump.

"I don't understand."

"It'd be a little eerie if you did," the cowboy says, pressing a worn button on the gas pump. The yellowish-green screen announces

THANK YOU. PLEEZ COME AGAIN

He pushes the "Clear" button. WELCOME TO PUMP-N-ZOOM. PRESS ANY KEY TO BEGIN

He shifts his weight from one leg to the other and pushes "zero."

PLEASE SELECT CASH OR CREDIT

Cash.

CREDIT OR DEBIT?

"God-damn it!" He jabs at "Clear" and starts over. The second time, he chooses cash and it accepts the answer.

PLEASE PAY CASHIER INSIDE. SELECT

The cowboy waits, ready to shoot the machine.

GRADE AND LIFT HANDLE

"Convenience." He unholsters the gas nozzle and realizes he's pulled the van up with the gas cap on the wrong side. After a good deal more swearing, Maggie intervenes and turns the van around for him. By the time the vehicle is properly repositioned, the pump has reset itself.

GAS PUMP MESSAGES DISPLAYED DURING FILL-UP:

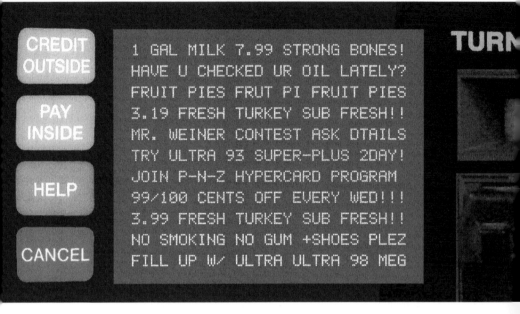

"**BEE! BOO!**" says the door.

Spaceman initiates a deliciousness scan of the premises, vectoring in on the fruit pie display. Cowboy sweeps the room with a cautious gaze. His assessment begins and ends with the boy behind the counter, uninterested in his customers, still reading *The True Adventures of Commander Hero and The Action Thunder Force*. Banjo peers around a candy display and mutters at Cowboy, pulling the boy's attention away from the epic battle with the sticky monster.

"Hey," the kid says. Customer service: Not his strong suit.

The cowboy leans in close to eye the comic book. "Glue-Belly, huh. What kinda name is that?"

"It's based on the real Commander Hero and his exploits!"

The cowboy snorts. "I bet."

Myron examines the man's holsters, his hat, his scarred face and strained eyes. "Are you... Are you a real cowboy?"

The cowboy shrugs and idly pokes at a Mister Weiner

# COMMANDER HERO

Commander Hero is a fictionalized character based on a real government contractor who fought to contain America's monster epidemic of the 1940s. A vast merchandising empire was later built upon his real-life monster-fighting exploits, including figurines, play sets, lunchboxes, comic books, and a radio drama. Rebranded in the 1980s as "Commander Hero and The Teen Esteem Team," the franchise dominated after-school cartoons and Sears catalogs for much of the decade. The property was reintroduced in the 1990s as "Commander Hero and The Action Thunder Force," a live action TV failure. A gritty reboot, *Hero Fallen: Rogue Vengeance,* will be released in theaters and streaming in 2021. The real-life Commander Hero is still alive and retired, identity and wherabouts unknown.

display on the counter, steering clear of the glaring little dog. "Where's th' bread? There?" He squints down the aisle, his eyesight blurring for a moment. "I see it. Never mind." He stomps away. Myron de-stools and follows the man down the aisle. Banjo hops off his shelf and joins them, nails clicking across the shiny tile floor.

"What should I get for Vampire?" Maggie asks Spaceman as she holds the refrigerator case door open with her hip. "Tomato juice?" *Ha-ha,* she thinks to herself. *Hilarious!* She balances a few bottles of water in one hand and a Coke in the other.

"He likes coffee," the spaceman replies. "We all like coffee. Black. Black coffee." He places a fruit pie into the store microwave, an ancient steel box encrusted with once-edible foodbits, and hits ONE ZERO ZERO ZERO START. The machine wearily cycles up to full power.

"He looked a tiny bit better this morning, huh?" she asks.

The spaceman shrugs. The vampire has rested in his coffin since the trailer park fire. Maggie helped him out of the van this morning so he could stretch his legs. He wore cheap sunglasses and a trucker hat* with "**I'M NOT AN IDIOT**" written on it. He teetered along the rest stop guardrail, sticking to the shade, leaning on a fancy cane. She has yet to hear him utter a single word.

"Stock up on water," the cowboy calls.

"What does it look like I'm doing?" Maggie snaps.

"Ohhhh! A *puppydawwwwwwwg!*" Spaceman falls to his knees and intercepts the little dog. "Whosagoodpuppadawg! *Youyouyouawwwwww!*" He twists the dog's excited face in his hands.

Myron eyes the short man in the spacesuit, his mouth hanging open. He works his jaw: "So you guys—"

"Here. Hold these," Maggie commands, forcing the pile of bottles into Cowboy's arms.

"Cripes, get a shopping cart or something, huh?"

*Shopping cart in a gas station convenience store. Where the hell is this guy from?* Maggie rolls her eyes and moves further down the aisle.

"So you guys," Myron begins again. "You guys are on an adventure, aren't you?"

"Here, kid. Put these on the counter, hah?" Cowboy passes the water bottles to Myron and follows Maggie.

"Who's the dog?" Spaceman asks the only dog in the room. "You!" he confirms. "*You're* the dog!" He skritches Banjo's snout and the dog leans into him. "C'mon, Chucklewagon!" He slaps his thigh like he's at some kind of goddamned hoedown. They run up and down the aisle.

"His name's... Banjo," Myron says in a small voice. He

---

* I don't know if wearing these things would effectively protect a vampire from the sun, but it's a thing he does, and it seems to work. I am not a vampire scientist.

heads back to the counter to drop off the bottles as instructed.

"So is there any medicine or anything we can get for Vampire?" Maggie asks.

"Just need to keep him comfortable," the cowboy assures her, scanning a shelf of overpriced bullshit. There is lots.

"Is that the whole plan?" she asks. He grunts.

"If you leave the true path," Spaceman whispers into the dog's ear. "You'll never cultivate right conduct." The dog throws his little body around in happy circles.

"So," Myron says as he jogs back up the aisle. "So you guys are... heroes? Superheroes?"

Maggie chortles and folds her arms. "Yeah, Cowboy. Are you guys superheroes or what?"

"Very funny."

"You're on an adventure, right?" the boy asks. "A hero's journey. Like *Lord of the Rings*."

"Sure, kid. Whatever." Cowboy rubs his eyes, his face, his jaw — an outward sign of frustration Maggie has come to recognize and relish.

"One puppy to rule them allllllll!" Spaceman tells the dog.

"Can I come with you? This place runs itself." Myron motions towards the store, the gas station, the town beyond. "They don't need me here."

"Kid," Cowboy says with a sigh. "What the hell would we do with you? We get ambushed and you're gonna give the bad guys incorrect change til they surrender?"

Myron's face cracks into a wide grin. "You *are* on an adventure! I knew it! C'mon, take me with you! I can help! I can!" The cowboy grabs him by the apron and spins him around. He pulls the comic book out of the boy's back pocket and whacks him on the head.

"Life ain't a comic book and this ain't an adventure!" Cowboy barks. He lets the comic drop to the floor. It falls open to where Myron left off. **HUBRIS!** declares Commander Hero. "And on toppa that you move slower than a plate of warm pudding."

"You're my best friend," Spaceman tells the dog. He puts his glass dome against the dog's head and makes a smoochy sound.

Myron is undeterred. This meeting is fate, his entry point into a vaster world. "Tell me about your adventure. Or is it a mission? Is it a mission?"

"Yes, Cowboy! I wondered that myself!" Maggie declares, hands on hips.

"Don't egg the kid on, hah?"

"What's the difference, exactly?" she asks Myron.

"Well, a m—"

"We're on a goddamned *adventure mission,* for shit's sake," Cowboy grumbles. "Now go sit on your goddamned stool."

Maggie laughs for the first time in a week. She examines the less-than-clean coffee maker next to the hot dog warmer. The former waitress dumps out the old coffee grounds and starts fresh.

"Customers aren't supposed to…" Myron trails off.

"Make one o' them for Vampire, huh?" Cowboy reminds her.

"No derr."

"Hah?"

"Vampire?" Myron says, mesmerized. "You guys gotta notsofartoo with you?" He points towards the cash register. "Someone came in yesterday with a flyer—"

The dog stands rigid, ears pointed at the ceiling tiles, his attention focused towards the front of the store. He barks once, a high, sharp yip.

**BEE! BOO!**

Spaceman reaches for the still-humming microwave. The cowboy slaps his glove away. "It's the door, stupid." Cowboy peers between bags of chips on a tall endcap. Three firemen enter the convenience store. He pushes Myron around the corner. "Go see what they want, kid."

Maggie crouches low as Myron mopes down the aisle. "What are we gonna do?" she whispers.

Cowboy thinks fast, or at least as fast as he's able. He rifles through the snack display in front of him, popping the top off a squeeze bottle of barbeque sauce. "You're gonna need to trust me on this." He bloops a glob into his hand and slaps his cheeks with the sauce.

"What is *wrong* with you?" Maggie whispers. He bloops another load and looks at her. "You're not." He smears her face with the thick brown sauce, pulling her close.

"Act normal," he murmurs.

"WH—"

He slides a sticky palm over her mouth. With his other hand, he squirts Spaceman in the helmet. Spaceman leans back, giggling and accepting the barbeque sauce *Flashdance*-style. "Maybe you should go get one of them slush-drinks," Cowboy says in a low voice.

"Slush Munkey! SLUSH MUNKEY!!! C'mon Snickerz!" The spaceman scrambles to the back of the store, the dog at his heels.

Down the aisle, Myron approaches his new customers. "Uh, hey. Can I help you?"

"Hey, sport. Hey, lil buckaroo." a fireman says. "Ya got any WD-40?"

Another asks: "Where are those, ahh, those three-hour energy spazz things."

The third wants six Mountain Dews.

Myron mumbles and points. Three squeaking pairs of Department-issued boots spread out into the convenience store.

Maggie makes an angry noise behind Cowboy's

## WD-40

The name WD-40 refers to the wildly successful 40th iteration of the chemist's water displacement formula. WD-39 was shit.

hand.

Cowboy lets go of her and points at his nose. "Tryin' to throw 'em off our scent," he says. "Now act casual." He picks up a can of self-heating instant latte from a nearby shelf and pretends to read the label. Maggie barks a single, incredulous laugh and grabs the coffee pot. One of the firemen strides up to her.

"Hi, there, I'm Ted!" the fireman says, one hand holding an ax, the other outstretched towards Maggie.

"H-Hi."

"That's Gary and Lewis." He motions behind Cowboy, where the other two firemen have squeaked up the aisle. Cowboy is engrossed in the instant latte label and doesn't look up.

"I'm Gary," says Gary.

"Hi, I know. He—"

"That's quite a daring makeup choice," Lewis says.

Maggie grins. "It's, ah..." Ted leans over her shoulder. She

## A BRIEF NOTE ON SELF-HEATING CANS

Many delicious beverages now come in heavy, nigh-recyclable cans, each consisting of an inner and outer chamber. When the activation button is depressed, unslaked lime (calcium oxide, or quicklime) is mixed with water in the outer chamber, triggering an exothermic reaction which heats the contents of the inner chamber to 145 degrees in around six minutes.

If accidentally punctured, the container can be quite dangerous, especially to animals and stupid children who like to play with punctured cans. This innovative product is marketed to the convenience-seeking, slothful urban consumer. Please consider purchasing as many of these wonderful beverage products as your household budget allows, and be sure to discard the empties in the nearest reservoir, state park, or bird's nest.

can hear him sniffing through his gasmask. "Ah, sunscreen."

"Sunscreen?" Lewis says.

"Very oniony," Gary nods.

"The SPF must be fantastic," Ted says.

BEEP. BEEP. BEEP.

Cowboy steps between Maggie and the firemen. "Excuse me, gentlemen," he says. He reaches into the microwave and lays his palm on Spaceman's fruit pie, which is approximately 800 degrees. "F██k of a goddamn!" The latte can clatters to the floor as he clamps his burned hand in his armpit.

"EEEEEEEE!!!" Spaceman barrels towards the microwave, helmet smeared with barbeque sauce and bright blue slush drink. He scoops up the molten apple pile with his gloved hands and runs off again. Banjo skitters in pursuit, slipping in the puddle of warming latte forming in the aisle. Cowboy stomps away cursing, looking for the ice machine.

Myron returns, frowning at Maggie's red-brown face. She smiles brightly at him, a slight tilt of the head that successfully communicates "Shut the eff up." She fills four cups with fresh, bad coffee.

"Uh, hey," Gary interjects in a fake-casual way. "You guys haven't seen any vampires or anything like that, have you?"

"Vampires?" she laughs. She fusses with a stack of to-go trays. "You're joking, right?"

Gary waves a gloved hand dismissively. "I know, right? We got a call from the Department. There was trouble a few towns over. Someone mentioned a vampire."

"And we were all like *whaaaaaaaat?*" adds Lewis. "Ha-ha!"

"Ha-ha!" Maggie glances out the front window at their RENT AMERICA! van and the old dull red pump truck parked next to it. Ted follows her gaze. She catches herself staring and blurts "Is that your, uh..." Oh, god. She's too far down this sentence's path now: "...truck?"

Ted does an overt double take. "That fire truck there?" Her cheeks burn. "Yes, ma'am. That is our fire truck." She shrugs and smiles. He points at his companions and himself. "Firemen and all."

Cowboy returns with an icy can of Coors cupped in his burned palm. He puts a hand on Maggie's elbow and moves her towards the exit. "Gotta get going," he says to the firemen. "It's been swell meeting you, uh, gents."

"Oh, likewise," Ted nods.

"I'm not sure this is working," she hisses.

"They're not that smart." Cowboy drops the rental truck key on top of the coffees. "Get to the van and wait for me," he mumbles. Louder: "Spaceman! Time to go!"

Spaceman runs to the front of the convenience store, the entire front of his spacesuit covered in hot pie filling. He faces the firemen, arms spread wide. "You can't see me," he whispers.

"Let's go, pal!" Cowboy shouts through his biggest, fakest grin.

"COME AHN! KILL ME! I'M HEAH! COME AHN! DO EET NOW!"

"I know that movie!" Gary exclaims. To Lewis: "I know that movie."

Cowboy's teeth are about to shatter. "Get in the f██king van, little fella!"

"Right on, Cowboy!" Spaceman shouts, giving his friend a double thumbs-up. Maggie ushers him out the door. **BEE! BOO!** The automatic door eases shut behind them.

Myron tugs at Cowboy's sleeve. "Take me with you!"

Cowboy spins the boy around and steers him towards the cash register. The firemen follow. "Listen, kid. You wanna be a hero? Get back behind that counter, ring us up, and zip your goddamned lip."

Myron is near tears. His chance, his escape, his dream is slipping away and cussing him out at the same time. *Even getting killed in some cool way would be better than this.* He fishes in his Pump-N-Zoom Express apron for the key to the cash register. "I need to charge you for the latte an' the pie an' the barbeque sauce an' the beer," the boy sniffles.

"What beer?" Cowboy looks down and sees the can still in his burned hand. "I don't want the goddamned beer!" He slams the Coors down on the counter and winces at the fresh bolt of pain.

"Well, I need to charge you for the coffees an' the gas—"

"Chrissake, fine!" mutters Cowboy, sensing Ted's gaze on the back of his head. He empties his pockets looking for money, slapping an assortment of change, lint, and receipts onto the counter, eventually finding a few crumpled dollars. "We're square," he states.

"Uh, okay," Myron whispers.

"You're doing good, kid," Cowboy says. "Keep 'em occupied til we're gone." He turns to leave.

"Back on the road, huh?" Ted asks. "All sunscreened up?" Cowboy nods. "You a cowboy or something?"

"You a cop?"

"Haw-haw!" Ted belly laughs. Cowboy taps his barbeque sauce-stained finger to the brim of his hat as a salute, circles around the demon, and pushes through the exit.

**BEE! BOO!**

Myron drags his shirt sleeve across his snotty nose, sifting through Cowboy's pocket debris on the counter. He unfolds a dogeared business card: velvety red with gold lettering: THE BROTHERHOOD. He squints at the flyer taped in the window next to the entrance. HAVE YOU SEEN A VAMPIRE? it reads. CALL US! - THE BROTHERHOOD.

The three firemen watch out the front window as the RENT AMERICA! truck rolls back onto the interstate.

"I dig that dude," Ted says, chuckling. "He seems like a reeeeaaal prick."

—◦◦◦◦◦—

# THE SOFT SHOULDER

MAGGIE DECIDES TO SAY A PRAYER. She isn't religious and never has been, but when you're locked in the back of a rental truck with a vampire and he's looking at you funny and there are demons fighting outside and all you have for a weapon is a small fireplace shovel, she figures you should consider biting the holy bullet and high-five Jesus, on the off chance he's actually up there paying attention.

"Everything's gonna turn out fine," Maggie whispers to Vampire. She can see him in the darkness of the back of the RENT AMERICA! van, sitting bolt-upright in his coffin, about five inches from her face, staring. They'd been taking a ten-minute stretch break on the side of the road when the firemen had ambushed them. Cowboy had shoved Maggie into the back of the van with the vampire and locked the door. He'd wanted to protect her, whether she was interested in being protected or not.

She can't hear much of what's going on outside. A muffled holler. Cowboy? Spaceman? Someone is slammed against the back of the van, a dull and far away thud. "I can fight if I need to," she whispers to herself. "I can do it. The firemen will break the lock and they'll come for us and I'll fight. I'll fight for us." Her voice is unsteady, her palms sweaty and gross. "But I'm sure they're doing just fine," she whispers to Vampire, who hasn't moved a muscle.

"Just fine," she repeats. She doesn't think they're doing just fine at all. What an odd thing to say. "Just fine," she repeats.

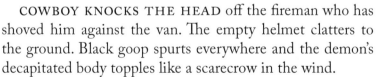

COWBOY KNOCKS THE HEAD off the fireman who has shoved him against the van. The empty helmet clatters to the ground. Black goop spurts everywhere and the demon's decapitated body topples like a scarecrow in the wind.

"Put me down! Put me down!" the Spaceman squeals at

two firemen holding him above their heads.

"We got the little fat one!" Doug cries to Chip.

"Little Fatty!" Chip sings.

"I'm not fat! I'm not fat!"

Cowboy takes a running leap at them, arms spread wide, and they all go tumbling over the guardrail and down the embankment beyond. They grapple in a dry creek bed, kicking up dust and ughing and oofing and cussing before the cowboy realizes he's punching Spaceman in the breadbasket and the firemen are already hustling back up the rocky slope. Doug is wearing Cowboy's hat.

"**Yahoo! Yahoo!**" the demon sings gleefully, making guns with his fingers. "**Pow! Pow!**"

"Stop that," Chip says.

The cowboy grabs the top of his head. Nothing but dandruff and sebum. "Sonofashit!"

"**Howdy, pardner! Howdy-do! Giddy-yup horsey!**" Doug dances a jig at the edge of the road. Cowboy picks up a rock and chucks it at the hat thief. It stings his burned hand something awful, and his throw is way off. *Bastard pie!* The firemen skitter over the guardrail and disappear from view.

> VOCAB-BUILDER:
> **Grapple** *(n.)*
> A brand name for a grape-flavored apple.
> No, I am not kidding.

"Aw, *hell* no!" The cowboy crawls over the fetal spaceman and scrambles up the riprap on all fours. He reaches the top in time to watch the demons sink into the loose gravel like a cheap special effect. They wave to the Cowboy. His hat exits this earthly realm.

"Don't worry about me!" Spaceman calls from the gully. "I'm okay! My suit is repairing my internal organs!"

"Open the door, Cowboy!" Maggie calls through the thick van walls. "What's going on?"

He touches the top of his head again. "Shit on me."

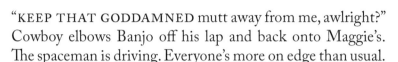

"KEEP THAT GODDAMNED mutt away from me, awlright?" Cowboy elbows Banjo off his lap and back onto Maggie's. The spaceman is driving. Everyone's more on edge than usual.

"Who's my little sailorpup??? You are! You, Piggybum!" the Spaceman coos. "This boat will never sink!" He squishes the dog's face.

"Eyes on the road, hah? Hands on the goddamned wheel?" Cowboy cradles his sore hand in his lap and mourns the loss of his hat. "Oh, I'll get it back, goddamnit," he vows to the dog-drool-smeared passenger window.

Maggie picks Banjo up and looks it in the eye. "Spaceman, why'd you steal that kid's dog?"

"I didn't!" the spaceman protests, letting go of the wheel and turning to face her. "Chucklehut followed me, I swear! He snuck into the van! I didn't even see him do it! I didn't even hide him behind the seat! He's just a smart little cheesedoodle!" He massages the dog's back. The van holds a steady course down the road.

"Jesus Chrysler, why is he driving?" Cowboy barks.

"You told him to so you could cry about your hat," Maggie reminds him.

"Can we stop for breakfast? Huh?" Spaceman asks. "Coffee? Some coffee?"

"Could you zip it?"

"Oh, leave him alone."

"Hungry?" Spaceman asks the dog. "You hungry, boy? Good girl!" He fishes around in his utility belt compartments. "I'm pretty sure I have dog snacks in here..."

Cowboy leans close to Maggie. "That hat's important to me, okay?"

"Next time we stop at a store," she says. "I'm buying you a tongue scraper."

The spaceman empties a selection of tablets out of the

spring-loaded box attached to his hip. "Food pellets! We eat these in outer space, Yip-Yip!" He offers a handful of pills to the dog, who swallows all of them. The dog whips Maggie in the face with his tail.

"What the hell is a tongue scraper?" the cowboy demands. "Is it gonna get me my hat back?" Maggie tries to seize the rogue dog tail. "I'm a cowboy. I need that hat. Cowboy without a hat? Never heard of such a thing. It's downright loco! Without it, I'm just a douchebag asshole nobody! Don't you know anything about cowboying?!"

She holds up a palm and turns her head away.

"I've had that hat a long time," Cowboy grumbles. He frowns, knowing the statement isn't precisely true. Where *did* that hat come from? He concentrates, but every time the thought seems within his grasp, a gust of wind blows it a little further down the road. He loses patience and pushes the topic away, down. He has to get that goddamned hat back. "Long time," the cowboy mutters.

"You guys have a real hang-up about costumes, you know that?" she scolds. "*Oh, I'm a cowboy! Oh, I'm a spaceman! Oh, I'm a vampire!*" she mocks in a high voice. "*Look at my cute little outfit!*"

"I ain't never said that!" the cowboy objects.

"Oh, I've said that," the spaceman nods. "I say that a lot."

Cowboy leans across the bench seat. "I need your commentary like I need earwax at a whisperin' contest!"

"Wow!" Spaceman gushes.

Maggie pushes Cowboy back to his side of the van. "You don't see me running around with an apron calling myself 'Waitress', do you?"

The cowboy scowls, scratching his jaw. "'Waitress' is a pretty good name."

"NO." She still has her order pad in her back pocket, but she keeps this tidbit of information to herself. It's for taking notes, honest.

**Beep.**

"What was that?" Maggie asks, tilting her head. "Did you hear that?" The spaceman says nothing, appearing to concentrate on the road ahead (he's actually watching a Jet Li movie* on his HUD). The cowboy mopes out the window. "It was a beep," she declares. She scans the dash, looking for a blinking light. Nothing. She looks at the dog sitting on her lap. She picks him up. "Did you hear the beep, doggie?" She turns to Spaceman. "What's his name again?"

"Sniffers," he says confidently.

"You don't know his name, do you?"

"Bagels?"

**Beep.**

Maggie arches an eyebrow and stares at the dog. She holds his belly against her ear.

**Beep.**

"Spaceman! *What* did you *feed* this *dog?*"

⊰•❧•⊱

COWBOY STEWS IN SILENCE, worrying about the dying vampire in his charge, the idiot spaceman on his nerves, and the waitress he feels he must protect. He glances at Maggie's neckline and sees the cheap gold cross around her neck. *Good. That's good.* At least he hopes it's good. To be honest, he doesn't have the slightest goddamned idea about vampire stuff. He worries about the Department and running out of money and bullets. He frets over his hat, his eyes, and his hand. He punches the dashboard. Hot pain shoots through his burned palm. Cowboy bites back a cry.

"What," Maggie snaps. "The hat? Are you seriously going to bring up the goddamned *hat* again?"

---

* An undubbed pre-1996 Hong Kong one, not any of that American crap.

"The cowboy hat, to a certain dead serious strain of cowboy, represents everything. While a cowboy without a six-shooter is merely a man who must steal some new guns, and a cowboy without a horse is simply a dude who needs a better pair of boots, what can be said of a cowboy without a cowboy hat? A cowboy without a cowboy hat is a douchebag asshole nobody. No Colt can change that, steel nor equine. Nor will a low-slung ammo belt, a cool Mexican serape, a hand-rolled cigarette, or a halfway decent squint. The cowboy hat confers identity and purpose to a cowboy, and no cowboy worth his salt would let someone take it away from him. A cowboy who allows his hat to be taken from him is a low man who has forfeited his own worth. Probably means he's super gay, too."

— EXCERPT FROM <u>MASCULINE HEADGEAR:</u>
<u>VIOLENCE, GENDER, AND HATS</u>
(1993, HOUGHTON AND SCHOOSTER)

"No!" the cowboy barks in protest. "I'll have you know I been thinkin' hard about the spot of trouble we're in and I'm trying to figure out how to get us out of it!" He taps the side of his head. "We need a master plan and I'm the masterplanner who's gotta masterplan it!"

"Really?" she asks, arching an eyebrow. "That's what's happening here? We're all helpless damsels and you're the only one who can save us?"

"I'm a boy damsel!" Spaceman declares. "A dudesel!"

"I'm just sayin'—"

"Oh, I'm *listening*, Cowboy. Please tell me *aaaaall* about your master plan for us." Maggie waits.

"My goddamned hat," he mutters.

"Oh, for christ's sake!" Maggie points out the window at an upcoming sign. "NEXT EXIT, SPACEMAN! WE'RE GOING TO

the mall

TWO CASHIERS grind against each other on a pile of cardboard in the Fashion Pig back room. A toddler runs head-first into the glass partition separating him from the two-story drop to the food court. A middle-aged couple enjoy a pleasant lunch at Pappa Za's Pizzaria. Maintenance receives a report of a large cat skulking around the dumpsters. I sift through the clearance rack at Old Navy, because I'll be damned if I'm going to pay full price for this crap. The toilet in the restroom near Ye Olde Christmas Shoppe spontaneously smears itself with shit. A man buys a pair of jeans without trying them on first. At ToyZone, an older gentleman deludes himself into thinking his grandson will enjoy a board game as a birthday present. Two women wait by the entrance of Teen Sizzle when the security alarm sounds. No one appears to assist them.

Cards are swiped, modems babble, accounts are debited, identities stolen, merchandise bagged, coupons redeemed, prices marked up, security tags removed, barcodes scanned. Transactions transpire. Commerce happens. The Meadowbrook Glen Mall happens.

———◦◦◦◦◦◦———

## LIFE

Milton Bradley's first board game, 1860's *The Checkered Game Of Life*, included a square marked SUICIDE.

Maggie leads her adventure mission companions to the mall's directory next to a cell phone kiosk. She scans the clothing section and sees a promising listing for a men's store called Mesa Diablo. As she searches for D-12 on the backlit map, Spaceman spins in circles and stares at the skylight.

"I'm humorin' you," Cowboy mumbles, supporting Vampire's elbow. The old man leans on his cane, his expression hidden by sunglasses. "I don't want no replacement hat."

"Tssst!" Maggie hisses.

The phone salesman accosts passing shoppers: "Hi, there, free phones. Cell phone. Free cell phone today. Hi. How are you doing today, ma'am? Free phone." His hair is slicked back and he's wearing a velcro phone holster on his belt and Maggie decides he is a pedophile or a date rapist because he works at a cell phone kiosk at the mall and has gross hair. She locates D-12 and steers her roadmates towards Mesa Diablo.

"Hi, there," the salesman says to them. "Free phones today." He holds out a Sangsonic non-smart phone. Spaceman reaches out. Maggie swats his hand away.

"No. Thank you," Maggie says through clenched teeth. She claps her hands. "Chop-chop, little onions!" she says, turning to her friends. "Let's go, people! Stay in a group!" They head deeper into the mall, coming up behind a Latina wearing a black miniskirt with the phrase

89

e the
ma
our
ma

written on the ass in electric pink Gothic letters. I can't afford the high-quality spot color process required to communicate to you, the reader, exactly how bright-electric-retina-burningly pink this text actually is, but trust me when I say the full effect is awe-inspiring and possibly transcendent. Transcendent of what, I do not know, and neither does Maggie, but it's difficult for her to avoid looking at this girl's ass. It is a magnet of attention, attracting eyeballs from all ages and all walks of life. It also dispenses valuable advice.

"Look at that lady's bum," Spaceman says.

Cowboy smacks him on the helmet. Vampire nods.

Maggie tears herself away from the booty wisdom. They join the human tide flowing down the main boulevard of the fictional hypertown. At the center of the mall, a circle of railing overlooks the food court two floors below. Across the chasm, Maggie sees the Mesa Diablo store front. The sign is written in the Papyrus font, which fills her with an indefinable-yet-palpable rage.

"That's the place," she says to Cowboy. Vampire stops short in front of FancyNails2000. Maggie pauses, a stab of apprehension in her guts. She frowns. "What—"

"What's up, old fella?" Cowboy grunts, following the vampire's gaze. A woman in a black jumpsuit stands in front of Mesa Diablo with two short, older men. The woman waits, arms folded, hip out, an exaggerated impatience. The men, in tweed suits and silly hats, hand out flyers to mall goers.

"Who are they?" Maggie whispers.

"Old trouble," Cowboy mumbles. "Best to avoid."

Spaceman humps a gigantic fiberglass M&M character in front of a candy store. "CAN WE GO TO JOHNNY HOTFAST HUH GUYS?" he yells. Cowboy snatches him down. They retreat into the sweet smelling store entrance and watch the strangers move towards the exit.

Cowboy exhales and turns to the Vampire. "Why don't you 'n' Spaceman go to the food court. "We'll meet you down there*."

Spaceman hops and shimmies, leading the Vampire towards the escalator. "Johnny HotFast is the ultimate 50's diner experience! They won't serve black people or anything!"

"Will those two be okay all alone?" Maggie asks.

"Will *we?*"

"Fair 'nuff."

They circle around to Mesa Diablo. It's twice as awful as Cowboy had suspected. A display case of silver hip flasks and aviator glasses greet them at the entrance.

"The hell is this joint about?" Cowboy asks.

"Outdoorsy rich white men who want to play Indiana Jones dress-up," Maggie says.

"A harsh judgment," the salesman says, circling around the counter. "But not entirely without merit."

"Oh, I'm sorr—"

He waves her off. "Absolutely fine, I assure you. I'm David. What can I help you with?" Cowboy prods at a rack of rainsticks. "I'm not sure we have those in your size."

"Hah?"

Maggie cracks up. Cowboy can't tell if he's the butt of the joke or not. He's tempted to use his last bullet.

"What we've got here," Maggie says, hands on hips. "Is a cowboy without a cowboy hat."

"An unacceptable predicament." David gestures towards the back of the store. "Hats are along the back wall, past the leather bomber jackets and the thousand dollar camp site espresso makers."

"Ooooh," Maggie laughs. "For roughing it!"

David nods. "Real survivalist stuff."

Cowboy steps between them. "Why don't you two stay here an' flirt so I can be disappointed in private."

---

\* In typesetting, a *widow* is a paragraph-ending line that falls at the beginning of the following page, separating it from the rest of the text.

"Cow! Boy!" Maggie cries after him, red-faced. David smiles at the carpet.

"Your boyfriend's funny."

"He is *not* my boyfriend. Be*lieve* me."

David looks up. "That so?"

COWBOY ASSESSES HIS CHOICES and longs to shoot himself in the face. The crisp-edged Liberty Valance rests atop a styrofoam head, a fat oil tycoon's hat for $900. Next to it: the Arroyo, the Ranchero, the High Noon. Hats not meant to be sweated in. Rich guy horseshit. The last hat in the display is a faux-distressed desperado hat named The Desperado. Cowboy scrapes at the patina on the artfully crumpled brim. Paint. $399.

"Jesus-nailed-to-a-coat-rack," he mumbles, his general disgust spilling over into personal offense.* "We're done here," he calls over a rack of authentic imported Mexican serapes and two thousand dollar boots. He stomps towards the exit. "DONE!"

"Uh..." Maggie says.

"Guess he's done," David nods.

"Sorry, he's—"

"—not the first cowboy to express displeasure in a Mesa Diablo, I assure you."

---

* I feel the same way about fashion models wearing Misfits t-shirts.

Cowboy pushes through a slow-moving group of elderly mall walkers and sulks by a coin-operated massage chair.

"I should go." Maggie takes a step towards the mall.

"Can I... Could I get your number?"

She flusters. As a waitress, she's used to being asked. She's not used to being interested. "I, uh... I don't have a phone."

"Oh, sure," David says, hands in pockets. "I get it."

She realizes how it sounds. "Oh. Oh! No! No, I really don't. It's not a blow-off. I don't have a phone. I don't even have a home, honest."

"Oh, jeez."

"Wait, that sounds weird, too."

"No, no—" David backs towards the counter. "You know, there's a phone kiosk down the—"

"I'm not homeless. Not that there's any shame in..." She waves her hands, trying to erase the conversation like an Etch-A-Sketch. "I mean I just don't have a place to stay right now. Or a phone." Maggie points towards the mall. "We're on a road trip."

"I think your cowboy is leaving you behind," David says. Cowboy is out of view.

"I should go."

He smiles. "It was nice meeting you, Maggie."

"Nice meeting you, too, David."

"Maybe stop in when you get back from your road trip."

She nods. "Maybe."

A tumbleweed bounces down the aisle. Wifi-enabled. $199.

---

# MYSELFISH

I SIT IN A MALL FOOD COURT. Well, I'm not actually in a mall food court, am I. I scribble notes for this scene on my porch in March, 2003. I'm on my living room couch in October, 2008 hammering this into outline form. I'm at the Montague

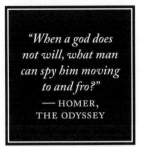

*"When a god does not will, what man can spy him moving to and fro?"*
— HOMER,
THE ODYSSEY

Book Mill in January, 2009 ballpointing a rough draft. At the library a week later, I edit the story and do research for a sidebar about Northampton. Suddenly, it's September. I complete a draft at a coffee shop, but then it's October and I'm back in my living room, re-thinking the whole project while I half-watch *Snakes on a Plane* on cable*. 2009 becomes 2010, and I'm in Turners Falls furiously editing.

Now it's 2015 and I'm in a different coffee shop. I no longer live in the house with the porch and the living room, and I just deleted the Northampton thing I worked so hard on six years earlier. Now it's 2016 and I'm at the library reconsidering the deletion of the Northampton sidebar, even though it isn't connected to the story anymore, other than being mentioned in this paragraph. I decree that this is reason enough to re-include it. Now it's half past 2017. Fourteen years compressed into two heavily-revised paragraphs. I am a time traveler, the lousy kind who can can only jump forward.

I sit in a mall food court. I take a few moments to settle into the self-caricature I've whittled for your entertainment. This version of me is intelligent, but imperfect; knowledgeable, but no god. This me may be relatively charming and quick-witted, but I take great care to share the good lines with the other characters, who are also me. This caricature is meant

---

* "Enough is enough! I have had it with these monkey-fried snakes on this Monday Friday plane!"

97

to be likeable. See, at my deepest core, I am a sad and lonely man. A pitiful crybaby of existential woe! Boo-hoo-hoo! I want the characters to like me. I want *you* to like me. I want you to totally wish you could hang out with me. We could rewatch *Freaks & Geeks*. I'm free Wednesday night. Call me.

# DEAR GOD LORD JESUS CHRIST PLEASE SOMEONE ANYONE CALL ME.

Ha-ha. I'm kidding, of course. Please never call me.

I sit in a mall food court, considering the god thing for a sec. I toy with the idea of levitating six feet above the french fry-covered floor. It would look pretty cool, but I don't write it. At the next table, a cell phone rings. A man answers and begins speaking loudly. I make his head implode. The result is horrific, more terribler than I have good adjectives for. Families are covered with brain and bone. There is screaming and confusion as the food court erupts into chaos. I undo the scene, and when the man's cellphone rings again, he wisely mutes it and lets it go to voice mail.

I sit in a mall food court. Eventually — or inevitably — my four main characters will descend the escalator to my left. They'll order some food at the food court's Johnny HotFast. I won't need to vie for the group's attention. They will come to me. There are only four available chairs in the whole joint, and they're at my table.

---

* A non-mainstream pop culture reference which will endear me to a particular subset of people. Like my earlier Jet Li reference, these are the tribal passwords of our times. Hey! You! *Firefly!* V66! Iron Maiden!

THEY APPROACH MY TABLE with their trays of burgers and coffee, eyeing my empty chairs. I do that thing where I raise my eyebrows and my chin at the same time. I say the word "Hey." I do this because I am incapable of speaking like an educated adult.

> *"I am an old man and have known a great many troubles, but most of them never happened."*
> — MARK TWAIN

"Mister, I d—" the cowboy begins, already protesting my impending invitation.

"Nah, nah. Come on. It's crowded. I saved you seats. I've been waiting. Sit." I move my laptop to make room for their trays. Spaceman sits down obediently, which annoys the hell out of Cowboy. The vampire ambles over to the table and sits. Maggie shrugs at Cowboy.

## NORTHAMPTON, MASS.

While today Northampton is best known for its lesbian and deluded artist population, the city was once the scene of an infamous miscarriage of justice. In the early 1800s, Dominic Dailey and James Halligan were accused of murdering Marcus Lyon of Wilbraham. The official charge was "Walking While Irish" (colloquially known as "Leprechaunism"), which carried the relatively heavy penalty of death by hanging. As the Northampton Police Department was not officially formed until 1884, it is presumed the two men were detained by the Northampton Society for the Detection of Thieves and Robbers, which is not a made-up name.

On June 5th, 1806, a Catholic priest from Boston, the Reverend Jean Louis Anne Magdeleine Lefebvre de Cheverus, condemned the crowd of 15,000 execution rubberneckers on Pancake Plain near Hospital Hill. "Oh! I blush for you," he admonished. "Your eyes are full of murder!" This is easily one of the raddest things a Catholic priest has ever said.

"Mighty kind of you," Cowboy says with an ill-concealed hint of resignation. They sit.

"That's a very cowboy thing to say," I respond. He chooses to take this as an insult. I have no preamble planned, so I jump right in. I lean forward and ask "Do you know who I am?"

"A crazy motherf███ker named Ice Cube?" Maggie ventures, warming her hands on her coffee cup.

"Wowwww! No waaaayyy!!!" Spaceman moons. "You're my favoritest actor!"

Cowboy shakes his head and takes a sip of coffee. "Hot damn!" he growls, impressed. "Strong enough to float a horseshoe." The vampire punctures his cup lid with his fangs and drinks deeply and solemnly from the wax-coated life-giver. Spaceman's cup is already empty.

"EEEEEEEEEEEEE!!!!" he squeals.

"Oh, is it good?" Maggie asks him. "Mine's wicked hot." She blows into the plastic lid drinky hole thing.

I clear my throat.

"I...

---

*(A dramatic pause goes here.)*

---

...am The Author." Somewhere, a church bell rings. The elderly clutch their brittle chests. Crows fall from the sky. The four people at my table ignore me.

Maggie sips her coffee and looks to Cowboy with an approving smile. "It's ridiculously good," she says. "It's delicious." She taps the coffee cup lid with her fingernail. "It's ridiculicious. Did I just make up a word?" Since when—

is food court coffee good?" It's good because I made it good.

"Whaddayoo write?" Spaceman asks.

*"Why, this Satan's drink is so delicious."*
— POPE CLEMENT VIII

"You," I say. I imagine a sudden orchestral stab underlining the massive magnitude of this reality-altering statement. I have a whole soundtrack planned out for this story, by the way. Deep cuts, man. I used to work at a friggin' *record store*. But we don't need to get into that now. Later. We'll get into it later. At this particular moment (somehow cruelly beyond my control), "Closing Time" by Semisonic plays over the mall sound system.

"Oh, yeah?" Maggie says absently. She's more interested in the coffee. She takes another sip.

Cowboy leans back in his chair and glances over his shoulder. Bad sight lines in this place. He motions to me with a gnawed coffee stirrer and says to his friends: "This dude's drunker than a fiddler's clerk."

I nod, accepting his mockery. "If a man drinks he's liable to go home and steal his own pants." Cowboy's smile fades a bit. "I copied both of those phrases out of a book about cowboys I read back in '97 or so."

"You don't got manners to carry guts to a bear, friend," he says (I copied that out of the same book\*\*). Cowboy taps

---

\* As of March, 2017, RIDICULICIOUS has 22,800 Google results (up from 6,380 in January, 2016). In the grand scheme of originality, this is a relatively small number of people, so let's just say Maggie and I made it up.

\*\* Other highlights: Crazy enough to eat the devil with his horns on. A ten-dollar stetson on a five cent head. If he closed one eye he'd look like a needle. Dead as a can of corned beef. So mean he'd steal a fly from a blind spider. Looked like the hindquarters of bad luck. He's so thin, he could bathe in a shotgun barrel.

the coffee stirrer against the table. "What else you think you know about cowboyin'?"

"Jack-shit. You started off as a writing challenge: *How do I make this dumb hero archetype interesting?*"

"And how'd you answer that?" Maggie asks.

"I had this idea, this thought," I say quietly. "What if the cowboy character *wasn't really a cowboy?*"

Maggie arches an eyebrow at Cowboy. "Buddy," he grumbles. "If you don't cut this horseshit, I'm gonna crack your walnut, comprendé?"

I totes com-pren-day. "Sorry, Cowboy. I'm kidding around," I say. "Don't go all new-cu-lar* on me."

He folds his arms and scowls 30% more than usual. Maggie jumps in. "So you're our author, huh?" she says brightly. "The heck does that mean?"

"You're all fictional characters," I say.

"I'm not a fictional character," Spaceman laughs.

"Yes you are," I assure him.

"OH MY GOD I'M A FICTIONAL CHARACTER!" he shouts in awe. The cowboy rolls his eyes. Maggie decides I'm the local weirdo, and adopts a placating tone.

"Okaaaay. You're our author. We're your characters." She smiles, not particularly engaged in the conversation. Her cup of coffee commands her attention. She wishes it would last forever. It technically could.

"I'm not crazy," I say, which is such a classic crazy-person thing to say. I mean, Christ, Tom. Come on. What are you thinking? "I made you all up." I motion towards the food court. "I'm making all of this happen. I've changed a lot of stuff around over the years, but this is basically this scene, happening right now."

---

* I mispronounce the word like George W. Bush used to, because sometimes I do that. It's important for me to reveal select personal flaws to you so you think you know me. This pseudo-intimacy bonds us. We are like kin now.

Maggie takes a too-big bite of her Johnny Hotfast Bel Air Burger. "Wait," she says, chewing. "You're saying there was stuff that was supposed to happen, but didn't?"

"No," I say. "I'm saying it *did* happen, and I made it *unhappen*." Cowboy snorts. He is a man who believes he is fully in control of his own destiny. I could change his mind, but I don't.

"So, you're all-powerful and stuff?" the spaceman asks. He waves a spoon in front of my face, hopping up and down in his seat. "Bend the spoon! Bend it!" It's silly he's asking, but it's even sillier because it's a plastic spoon.

I lean in close and whisper, "There is no spoon."

This blows Spaceman's mind. "*Whoooooooaaaaaaaa!*" Maggie snorts. But seriously, there is no spoon. Right?

I want Maggie to ask me how long I've been working

---

## CLOSING TIME

Semisonic's 1998 radio hit was released in several different versions to appeal to different radio listening demographics:

**THE TOP 40 MIX** — More tambourine, quieter guitars

**ALT ROCK MIX** — Louder drums, more electric guitar

**ADULT CONTEMPORARY MIX** — The promo-only cassingle came packaged with a free box of white wine.

**HORRORCORE JUGGALO MIX** — More suicide and rape references; face paint

**NEGRO SPIRITUAL MIX** — Louder ring chants, sweeter and lower chariots

**BIG BAND NU-SWING SKA-FUNK METAL MIX** — More commercial pandering; trend█king

on the story so I can answer her. "How long have you been working on your story?" she asks.

"Long time," I say. "Ten or twenty-three years or so."

"Why'd it take you so long to write it?"

I sit back. "When you write, that story is linked to who you are as a person in that moment. But if time passes and you're still tinkering with the same story, you end up on a Möbius strip of endless rewrites, forever adjusting the old text to reflect the person and writer you've become."

"Deep." Cowboy grunts as he chews on his burger. "You write that?" Maggie kicks him under the table.

"I'm afraid to give up control of this world, to stop manipulating little details of it. I'm afraid to set it loose, to let it *be*. What if my next world isn't as good as this one?"

Cowboy rolls his eyes at the food court. "Yeah, quite the wonderland you've chucked together here."

"Everything is so *detailed!*" Spaceman declares, studying the Johnny HotFast tray liner, which is blank.

Maggie smiles into her cup lid. "So you've been working on this for a long time?"

"I started this as a comic in, like, 199—"

"Jesus Chocolate Chip Christ on a cookie cross," Cowboy interjects. "You created us, huh? So if you died — and by that I mean 'If I kill you right now' — we'd cease to exist or something, yeah?"

"Well, no," I say, contemplating the question. "I've already created you. But if I died you'd cease to *continue*. You'd be stuck in this food court with my dead corpse for eternity. This conversation would never end. Time would stop."

I open my laptop and update my Facebook status: *is talking to himself again.* * I close the browser and open PowerPoint. "I

---

* Remember when people phrased their Facebook status updates in third person, with their username read as the first words of the sentence? I wrote this bit in May, 2009. Tom Pappalardo was younger then.

wanna show you guys something," I say.

"Aw, *helllll* no!" Cowboy cries. He kicks his chair back and steps away from the table. "C'mon. Let's go." His friends remain seated.

"You'll want to see this, Cowboy," I explain. "I've got notes on symbolism and themes, character backgrounds, all kinds of stuff..." I hold the laptop in front of his face:

## Cowboy - character notes/questions

- **Total ripoff of Roland from *Dark Tower***
- **Vampire = Father figure? Who is saving who?**
- **A flawed hero in decline (older, injured, fragile ego)**
- **Is Cowboy really in charge? Why?**
- **Connection to Spaceman? The firemen?**
- **Unanswered questions (for later):**
    - **How long was he walking in desert?**
    - **Where did that sword come from?**
    - **Does he not remember his past, or has he chosen to forget it?**
    - **Who was Cowboy before he stole that hat?**

He glares at me with a dark and serious look, the dead-eyed stare of a Richard Scarry cat piloting a tugboat. "We're done here," he says, closing the laptop before the others can see.

Maggie motions towards the Vampire's half-eaten DelRay Deluxe Burger with Powerglide Sauce. "We've gotta eat, Cowboy. What's your problem?"

"I'm goin' back to the van. Y'all come along or don't." He heads for the escalator. Spaceman hops out of his chair and chases after him.

"IT WASN'T SUPPOSED TO HAPPEN LIKE THIS," I say. "I scripted out this big cool interaction between us. I had the whole PowerPoint thing planned out." I point at my laptop, the scuffed, half-broken machine that was brand-new when I wrote the first draft of this paragraph. It will probably die before this story is published.* "I worked super hard on the page transitions," I say to myself, which is no different than talking to Maggie, or talking to you. I scratch at my beard. Has it always been this white?

"Sorry," she says. "Cowboy can be a bit..."

"Dickish. I know," I say. "He has limited social skills. I tried my best but—"

"Listen, Arthur. It was nice meeting you. Really."

"Author."

"Yeah, good luck with your book. But we should get going." Vampire pushes his chair back. The scraping sound in the echoey, tiled mastication pit is the worst sound on the planet.

"Maggie," I say. She doesn't even notice I know her name. "You can go back, you know. Back to a regular life. You don't need to ride around in the van with us, with them. New job, new apartment, new life. I can do that for you, if you'd like." I don't know why I want to offer her an out, but I do. No one deserves to be stuck in one of my stories. This gal needs a hall pass. A Get Out Of Prose Free card. "You could hook up with that David guy. You could get Mr. Kittywhiskers back." I add.

A pang of loss hits her in the gut. "Kitty!" she moans. She thinks about riding around in the van. The bad food and shit coffee and cramped quarters. The rest stop bathrooms. She thinks about the line between Good and Evil. She thinks about the fragile Vampire trying to get home, the odd Spaceman, Cowboy. Maggie stands. "It's a nice offer, hon. But I've got a job to do. These guys need me."

Vampire winks at me as he rises, key ring jangling.

---

* It did.

"No!" I plead. "Don't you see? This is supposed to be a big-deal turning point in the story! I've got to reveal a bunch of important junk* to help you!"

"Okay, so how does it end?" Maggie asks, arms folded. "Your story. Our story. How does it end?"

I mull that for a sec, trying to sum up the end of the story I've been working on for almost half my life. I open my manila folder, but there are too many crossed out bits, arrows, and notes scrawled in the margins. I fiddle with a binder clip. "Death and disappointment," I say.

She looks at the vampire. The old man taps his cane against my sneaker. It's a fancy carved hunk of deep red wood. Pretty as hell. He hobbles towards the escalator. Maggie says goodbye and follows.

I shove all my crap back into my laptop bag, jamming it in, pushing it down. "It wasn't supposed to happen like this," I sigh to myself. I'm older than I thought I'd be, back when I was drawing comics and stapling them to telephone poles, back when Phil Hartman was alive, back when my dad was alive, back before my breakup and breakdown, before I had an email address or knew what recycling was. "It wasn't supposed to happen like this at *all*."

> * Douche
> ex machina

I sit in a mall food court, The Author, the Big Whoop Author. I slouch in the spine-destroying metal chair and wait for this painful chapter of my life to end.

*"Running looooowwwwwwww."*
— IRON MAIDEN,
HALLOWED BE THY NAME

# PART THREE

## Tribulations & Coffee

IN WHICH OUR HEROES ARE
SEPARATED, WHICH IS A THING
THAT HAPPENS IN A LOT OF OTHER
STORIES, TOO. ALSO, A TALE FROM
THE DESERT.

# EXEUNT

**H**IGH ABOVE THE MEADOWBROOK GLEN MALL PARKING LOT, four thousand pigeons cram behind the metal letters of the west wing entrance, competing for space on a narrow strip of poop-covered aluminum flashing. Cowboy storms out of the mall, grumbling about PowerPoint and smart-ass college boys. He senses he's somehow lost control of things: the people in his charge, his mission, his damned hat. He is unsure. He doesn't like feeling unsure. Spaceman pushes through the glass doors, clutching a large teddy bear dressed like Charlie Brown.

"Where in *hell* did you get *that?*" Cowboy asks in disbelief.

Spaceman points over his shoulder. "You can build your own bear at that place. Greate-A-Griz. I gree-ated it." He holds the teddy bear up to Cowboy. "It's Ziggy. From the funnies."

"How'd you—" Cowboy squeezes the bridge of his nose in frustration. "You stole that, didn't ya? Jesus, what part of low profile don't you understand?"

"Both parts."

"Don't be a smart-ass."

"I wasn—" Cowboy shushes him with an open palm across his helmet. Beyond a nearby SUV, a lone fireman leans against a Corvette. The fireman runs his gloved hand along the door trim, which begins to smoke. Cowboy takes no notice of this. He's focused on the fact that the fireman is wearing

# "MY HAT!"

"Gyaah!" Doug flinches. Cowboy charges forward, grabbing Doug by his narrow throat. The fireman clamps himself around Cowboy's waist and pushes them both against a light pole.

"BAUUFFFF!" Cowboy exhales. His Remington tumbles out of its holster and clatters across the asphalt.

"Hold on, Cowboy!" Spaceman cries. "I can help!" He jabs at the keypad on the back of his left glove, unwilling to relinquish the teddy bear. "Laser Armageddon Collider: ACTIVATE*!" he shouts. He pushes buttons for food and navigation coordinates and atmospheric readings. The MECH-9 tries its best to figure out what he wants. Doug slams Cowboy against the smoldering Corvette's hood. "Stand back, Cowboy! I got it!" Spaceman aims his glove. "GO POWER GLOVE 3000!" The MECH-9 hums ominously.

"Yeep!" Doug cries. He retreats downward, dropping into the parking lot.

"Not again, amigo!" Cowboy hollers. He grabs Doug in a headlock and they sink together. The otherworld swallows them both.

"Cowboy?" Spaceman calls, arm still raised. His suit's Main Propulsion Cluster activates and throws his little body into the sky.

---

RETURNING TO THE RENT AMERICA VAN A FEW MINUTES LATER, Maggie and Vampire find an abandoned teddy bear and a half-melted Corvette.

"I think we just missed something," she says quietly. She spies Cowboy's revolver under the rear tire of a Prius and grabs it. Behind them, the mall fire alarms sound, blaring inside and out. She spins around, gun raised. Smoke escapes from the skylight over the food court. *Firemen.* Vampire steps around the teddy bear and continues to the van. "Where are you going?" she asks. "Cowboy and Spaceman might still be

---

* That's not a thing.

inside!" He takes off his hat and shakes his head 'no.'

"How do you know?"

Vampire points at a burn mark on the asphalt and taps on the passenger window, prodding her to unlock the door. She squints at the mark on the ground. *Spaceman?* She looks up at the sky, trying to peel back clouds and layers of atmosphere* to reveal her little friend. *Where the hell did you guys go?*

Mismatched ladder trucks pull up in front of the mall's main entrance. No lights, no sirens. The Department. Maggie turns to the vampire. "There are people in there," she implores. He taps the window again, while Banjo squishes his face against the dog nose-smeared glass and barks. Maggie watches the firemen hustle into the mall, dragging a long firehose behind them. She knows the gun in her hand isn't enough. One bullet isn't enough. She isn't enough.

Often in popular film and literature, weather is only mentioned as either an obstacle to be overcome or as an emotional mirror, giving the audience an overt cue that things must be bad for a character, because, *fer cryin' out loud, it's raining!* It's a bit of a literary underline, I guess. At this point in our self-referential, post-modern, hyphenated-phrase culture, it seems a bit overdone to me. Like it's important for me to prove to you, the reader, that yes, I've totally seen *Seven Samurai,* and yes, I totally watched the commentary track on the Criterion edition.

Anyway, it starts raining wicked hard.

# *THE ATMOSPHERE

While many believe atmosphere to consist of dim lights, candles, and smooth jazz, the Earth's outer layers of gases are in fact a complex and important system supporting our continued existence on this planet.

**Outer Space** - F█kin' wormholes and shit

**Inner Space** - Martin Short, Dennis Quaid, Meg Ryan

**MySpace** - I don't think there's anything there at all

**Thermosphere** - The one Al Gore used to always talk about, I think

**Ionosphere** - Influences radio propagation

**Ione Skye** - This is where the word "sky" comes from

**Stratosphere** - A velvety dark curtain swaddling the planet at night, with holes poked in it to let starlight through. Placed there by the ancient mystics, The Stratocasters.

**Blogosphere** - A thick layer of complaining that helps protect the planet from harmful STFU Rays

**Troposphere** - Where farts and bad breath commingle

*Source:* Space Agency

# HIGH

SPACEMAN SOARS through a layer of storm clouds, accelerating like a son of a bitch. His suit propels his body away from Earth at a lung-crushing velocity. The sound of the wind against his helmet is deafening.

"ZIGGGGGGGGGGGGGYYYYYYYYYY!!" he moans. His HUD illuminates the inside of the helmet glass, crowding his field of vision with a scrolling blast of numbers and statistics. He has seen displays like this before, especially when he hits a bunch of buttons, but this time seems particularly blinky. An old episode of his favorite TV show, *Mighty Power Cats*, appears in a popup window. Felinedra casts a spell on a zombo-dog, who begins breakdancing uncontrollably. The show blocks his view of the clouds whizzing past him, which is sort of annoying.

"TV off! *Mighty Power Cats* delete!" The MECH-9 does not acknowledge him. "Cats no! *MPC* off!"

The HUD responds:

> VOICE COMMAND INPUT: MPC OFFLINE

At the same moment the Space Agency's Rogue Hardware Retrieval unit detects his location, the MECH-9's Main Propulsion Cluster powers down and the spaceman ➤

drops like a rock.

(This is the sort of thing that might alarm Spaceman, but fortunately he faints immediately.)

# THE LANDING

COWBOY LIFTS HIMSELF off the floor of the chamber. The dim cinderblock room is lined with rows of hooks holding a variety of firefighter coats and helmets. An equally varied assortment of heavy boots are piled beneath the hooks. In the center of the room, a brass fireman's pole leads from nowhere to nowhere. Doug stares at Cowboy with his arms folded. Four other firemen stand behind the demon, blocking the room's lone exit. Cowboy sighs and picks his hat up off the floor. He slaps it against his thigh, raising a cloud of dust.

"Welcome to Department headquarters," Doug says.

Cowboy pulls his hat down over his eyes. "Ah, hell," he mutters.

| 72% | 58% | 71% |
|---|---|---|
| of Americans believe in Heaven. | of Americans believe in Hell. | of Americans believe in Black Sabbath's 1980 album *Heaven and Hell*. |

*Pew Forum on Religion & Public Life, 2014*

# BOOGIE ON

THEY DRIVE THROUGH THE NIGHT. Maggie focuses on the interstate, keenly aware of the lack of arguing in the van. Banjo snoozes between the vampire's feet while the old man fiddles with the radio. She doesn't let him pause on any news reports. She can't bear to hear anything about the mall, if there was a fire, who was hurt. There is shame deep in her gut. It was shit odds, but she should've stepped up, right?

For the third time in as many hours, the radio plays a

Stevie Wonder song. "Boogie On, Reggae Woman" funks out the door speakers. Maggie fears Stevie has died and all of the radio programmers have rushed to broadcast his music as a memorial. Maybe it's his birthday? Maybe it's just a coincidence. She doesn't have the emotional bandwidth to deal with a celebrity death right now, goddamnit.

The moving van crests a hill and Maggie spots a state trooper with a radar gun trained on them. Her grip on the hand-gunk-coated wheel tightens. *Speed trap!* The RENT AMERICA! van, sheilded with top secret stealth technology, passes like a ghost while the trooper frowns at his device. Maggie slows down, double nickels on the dime, while Stevie and the mall and her missing friends weigh heavily on her worry list.

*Cowboy and Spaceman. They'll catch up*, she reassures herself. She has no idea how, since they don't know where she's going, because she doesn't know where she's going. Somehow she's reassured anyway. It'll work out. The old man sits next to her, still as a fence post, eyes forward. Maggie hears another muted beep from the sleeping dog's belly. "Too many prawwwblems," she sings in a flat monotone. "We're all f█████cked."

## RADAR

Radar (Radio Detection and Ranging) bounces radio signals off an oncoming vehicle. The return frequency is different than the originally transmitted radio signal, and that difference determines the vehicle speed (frequency shift). Radar guns are calibrated by sound, using a standard tuning fork. To prevent the cops from getting a reading on you, sing an A# as loud as you can.

# LOW

SPACEMAN WAKES UP from a suborbital fall, his body sore, his senses scrambled. He can't move — totally stuck or something. His helmet is pressed against a large rock. A little upside-down fish swims past. Spaceman suspects he's stuck at the bottom of the ocean or maybe in a fancy aquarium. The HUD awaits his order.

> **COMMAND LINE _**

"Am I upside down?" he asks the suit. His voice sounds thick and goofy to his ears.

> **AFFIRMATIVE.**

"How long have I been here?"

> **TWO HRS FOURTEEN MIN NINE SEC AT TONE.**

A doorbell sound rings in his helmet. Surround sound. "Where am I?"

> **PENOBSCOT RESERVOIR. SITE OF FORMER TOWNSHIP OF PENOBSCOT, DISINCORPORATED APRIL, 1938, FLOODED MAY, 1938. YOU ARE NEAR THE INTERSECTION OF MAPLE AVENUE AND HEBERT LANE. YOU ARE AT THE BOTTOM OF A WELL.**

The spaceman peers at his limited view. "How deep am I?" Cross-referencing its keyword database, the MECH-9 suit replies with a mostly not-applicable passage from *Richard III*. Quoth the HUD:

### Had you such leisure in time of death To gaze upon these secrets of the deep. *

"Oh."

The spaceman waits for something else to happen, but nothing else happens. He waits a while longer. Like, half an hour. But he doesn't know that for sure because the heads-up display doesn't have a clock. You'd figure it would, but it

---

\* At this point in the narrative it should be explicitly stated that the MECH-9 spacesuit is a little eccentric and doesn't actually work that well.

doesn't. One thousand hidden functions, no clock. "I wonder what Cowboy's doin'. I wonder what Vampire's doin'. I wonder what... that lady's doin'." No response from the HUD or the reservoir or the little fish. He is alone. He sighs. "I wish I had a game to play."

> **RUNNING QUERY: GAMES ...**

> **SEARCHING...**

> **RETRIEVING...**

> **SELECT FROM MENU:**

> **1. THERMONUCLEAR WAR**

> **2. 3-D CHESS**

> **3. MAGIC 8-BALL**

> **4. ESCAPE FROM THE WELL AT THE**
>    **BOTTOM OF THE RESERVOIR**

> **5. PIRATE TEXT-BASED ADVENTURE**

"Ooooh!" the upside down spaceman coos. "Pirates!"

---

## ALL MAGIC 8-BALL RESPONSES, ALPHABETIZED

| | |
|---|---|
| AS I SEE IT, NO | OUTLOOK GOOD |
| ASK AGAIN LATER | OUTLOOK EXPRESS |
| CANNOT PREDICT NOW | QUIT RELYING ON BALLS |
| DON'T COUNT ON IT | REPLY HAZY, TRY AGAIN |
| NOT LIKELY | YOU'RE SO HIGH RIGHT NOW |
| NOT F██KING LIKELY | YOUR LIFE IS A CRUEL JOKE |

---

# EVIL

THE HALLWAY IS POORLY LIT AND HUMID. Water-stained drop ceiling, floor tiles thick with dulled floor wax. Cowboy is escorted past heavy wood doors, scuffed from years of careless use. He's pretty sure this is Hell because this joint is a dead ringer for a public high school he visited once.

"Time to meet The Chief," says Doug, halting Cowboy in front of an unmarked door.

"You're in for it now," says Chip, trying hard to sound super-serious.

"You are soooooooo super-dead," adds Doug.

"Totally dead!" agrees Chip with a vigorous head nod.

"Ya scared?" teases Doug. "You should be. He's our leader. The Chief is the manifestation of Evil. He is pure, distilled treachery. We made him."

"Couldn't care less,'" Cowboy says.

"He is extremely evil."

"Sure."

"Hey, Doug," Chip asks. "Do you suppose this cowboy dude's gonna get his ass handed to him?"

"Well, you know, Chip," Doug mock-deliberates. "Ummmm, I am thinking the answer is 'yes'!" They high-five.

Cowboy rolls his eyes. The two demons laugh too hard.

"Reckon I'm in a real jam-jar," Cowboy sighs.

"It's true. Get ready for some dark shit, my man."

"It's hot enough to melt clabber in here," Cowboy complains. "Put a burr in your shoe and open the gaddamn door, hah?"

"This isn't as fun as I'd hoped it'd be," Doug pouts.

The fireman knocks and opens the door.

—◦◦◦◦—

* There is a great debate raging across this great land of ours. No, not hard-G versus soft-G "GIF" pronunciation (I got you a birthday jift: It's a hard G. Deal with it). I'm talking about the "could care less" versus "couldn't care less" rift that threatens the very foundation of our republic.
I'm a longtime a fan of "I could care less." I hear it as a lethally sarcastic comment, essentially telling a person "I have the *capacity* to care less about you, but you *don't even deserve that much effort or attention, so I'm not going to bother.*" Think about it. It makes sense, and it's super-mean. THAT'S ME.

THE ODOMETER ticks off miles. They pass big box stores and RV dealerships and water treatment plants that look like sets from bad sci-fi movies. As she passes a sagging Camry, Maggie gets a swift and pure hankering for coffee. A black coffee in a big to-go cup. She can picture it, a grail floating in the clouds, holy light radiating towards the heavens. Her desire is clear and specific, which strikes her as odd since she's a cream-and-sugar kind of lady. She frowns and considers pulling off at the next exit. Maybe she needs a break.

The vampire exhales, an affectation of the undead, and points at the chain around Maggie's neck. "This?" she says, embarrassed by the obviousness of the thing. She pulls the cross out from her collar and lets it rest on her shirt front. "It's nothing. I'm not religious. Cowboy gave it to me. It's nothing. No big deal."

Vampire reaches for it. "Should you do that?" she asks. "I thought, um, you know. The whole cross thing was like, bad or something? For guys… like…you?" He touches the cross. A sizzling sound and the smell of burning leaves. He smiles

serenely, eyes silvery and blank. "Stop that!" She jerks away from him, sending the van veering across the double line.

"Why did you do that?" she demands. "Why would you do that? Are you nuts?" He holds up his finger. The image of the cross fades from his fingertip. "You're weird, you know that?" His smile turns into a toothy grin. Very toothy.

The little dog whimpers, nudging the vampire's wrist with his snout. Maggie rubs her eyes, a humdinger of a headache coming on.

"Yeah," she confirms. "I think he has to poop, too." Maggie frowns at the old man. They pass an 18-wheeler, a minivan with a faded 9/11 bumper sticker scotch taped to the rear window, a Honda Civic with a mismatched fender. "Hey," she says, tilting her head. "I think it's time you and I stopped for a cup of coffee."

The vampire brightens up.

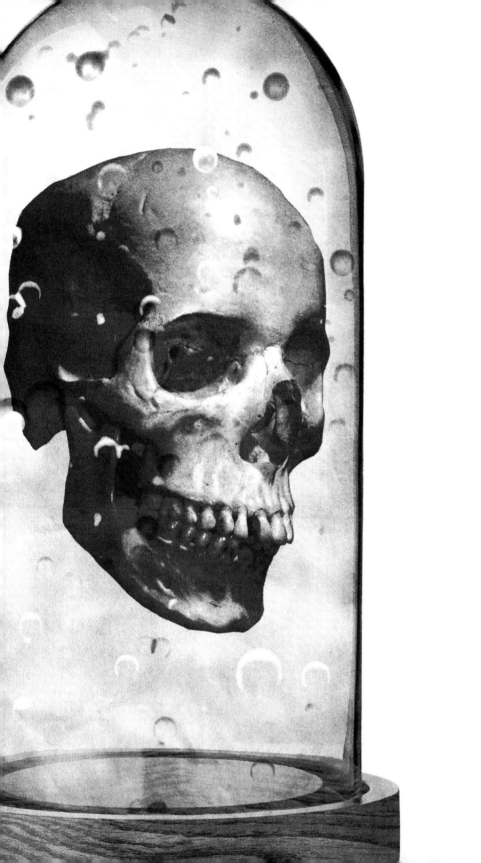

# THE CHIEF

"WELCOME," the skull says. Its voice is roupy and low, grating on Cowboy's ears like a stuck drawer full of screws and batteries. Cowboy stands in the doorway, offering no reaction to the glass dome perched on the edge of the desk, nor the skull floating inside it. The Chief gets annoyed when people act like they're not surprised.

*"It is not my intention to be fulsome, but I confess that I covet your skull."*
—DR. MORTIMER, THE HOUND OF THE BASKERVILLES

"You're one of the troublemakers, huh?" he asks.

"I'm wont to trouble-make, I reckon."

The Chief frowns. "You're the vampire?"

Cowboy snorts and gestures to his clothes. "Yeah, I'm a vampire cowboy. That makes sense. I'm a chef, too." The firemen laugh.

"Stop it!" Chief shouts. "Don't laugh at his jokes!"

"Sorry, Chief."

"What's your problem, Good Guy?" the Chief asks, swishing around his jar. "Why do you keep meddling with our business? You some kinda macho asshole that hates evil?"

"Amigo, you just wrote my epitaph."

"Lines like that are why people hate cowboys."

"That so."

"Yes, it's f█king so! Chip! Hit him!" Chip steps forward and delivers an open-palmed whack to the back of Cowboy's head. It annoys Cowboy. "Doug! Kick!" Doug kicks him in the shin.

"Ouch, gorramnit!" the cowboy hollers.

"Not so cocky now, eh, Good Guy?" The Chief cries. "Welcome to a world of agonizing and everlasting woe, hero!"

Henry knocks on the open door and holds up a mug.

"*Coffee tiiiime!*" he sings.

"Not *now*, Henry!" The Chief seethes.

"I got a bullet reserved for you," the cowboy growls,

rubbing his leg.

"Ooooooooohhh!" The Chief mocks.

"Ooooooooohhh!" Doug parrots, wiggling his fingertips.

"So you just go around fighting evil, is that it?" The Chief asks.

Cowboy shrugs. "Same as you, I suppose. Just the opposite." He scratches his chin. Fair amount more stubble than he had this morning.

"We've got big plans. Big evil plans. I don't need these penny-ante interruptions," the Chief complains. "You come down here, for what? Some kind of attack? Sabotage? Infiltration? What?"

"Just wanted my hat."

The Chief squints.* "Who is this hick?" he asks Henry. "Why are we talking? Is this the guy giving us trouble or what?"

Chip sniffs Cowboy's shoulder. "He's got our smoke on him, Chief. He's marked."

"I don't have time for this. Henry, do I have time for this?"

Henry leans forward and flips through the Chief's desk planner. He makes a clucking sound with his tongue as he scans the week. "You don't have time for this, Chief. Meetings all afternoon."

"Meetings," the Chief grumbles. "I didn't sign up for *meetings*, I'll tell you that."

"You didn't sign up for anything, Chief. 'Member?" Henry says.

The Chief's expression darkens.

"Can we move this along?" Cowboy asks.

"Intercom!" the Chief demands, impatiently swishing around in his jar. Doug doesn't move fast enough, so the Chief demands it again, except louder, preceded by the word "f█king" and followed by the word "now." Doug hustles

---

* How, exactly, I'm not sure.

forward, kicking aside a few errant three-ring binders, and presses a button on a plastic box on the desk. Feedback squeals through the room and echoes down the hallway. Cowboy winces. The Chief hollers at the box: "We're throwing a cowboy chef into the pit!"

# DUNK-A-DONUT

MAGGIE ESCORTS VAMPIRE into **DUNK-A-DONUT** as the sun sets beyond Exit 15. Every surface inside the franchise is colored orange or brown. She is assaulted by logos, on the cups, shelves, windows, wallpaper, and cardboard displays. The workers, too.

A retiree with a white captain's hat sits at a window stool. He nurses a small senior discount coffee. Maggie christens him *Cap'n Grampy*. He nods at Vampire and Vampire nods back. Old man secret handshake. The vampire eases into a booth while Maggie orders a couple of coffees. Terrible pop-country drawls over satellite radio while the TV plays candlepin bowling on mute.

"I'm worried. The dog won't poop," Maggie says, sitting down. She slides a styrofoam cup towards him. "Black." He runs his fingernails over the sides of the cup, lightly, a caress. "I mean, I'm not sure he *can* poop. We might need to find a vet." This thought triggers worries: Credit cards, I.D.s, appointments, bills. It's a reflex, a fight-or-flight response to modern American life. She exhales slowly. That life is done with now. A ghost limb, a half-remembered sitcom.

Cap'n Grampy swivels on his counter stool. "This your daughter?" he asks Vampire.

"I'm not his daughter," Maggie answers. The Cap'n smiles and nods. He taps on the glass, motioning towards the RENT AMERICA! van parked out front.

"That your van?"

"It is, indeed."

"Where you moving?"

"Haverford," she says. It's a town name she'd seen on a sign* a few miles back.

"Almost there," The Cap'n says. "Real nice up there."

"Mmmm-hmmm." She feigns interest in televised bowling. The closed captioning says

**DOUBLE WORKING: FOURTH FRAME. TOUGH SPLIT.**

Cap'n Grampy swivels back to his coffee cup.

"It's been a lonely couple of days on the road with no one to talk to," she tells Vampire. "I mean, with no one talking back. No offense." He dismisses her worry with a little wave. *No problem.* She taps the side of her to-go cup. "If you could talk, I'd be able to ask you where you came from, how long you've been..." She gestures at his cloak. "Vampiring." He sips his coffee. It is blacker than his cloak. "I'd ask you how you hooked up with Cowboy, and how Spaceman factors in." She swishes her cup out of habit, a hand motion to mix her sugar and cream and coffee. But this coffee is black. Blacker than a vampire's cloak.

"I know a fella named Sam from Haverford," The Cap'n interrupts. "Drives a green pickup?"

"Don't know him," Maggie answers.

The Cap'n nods. "He's up at the VFW plenty. You need a stump pulled, you call him."

Maggie leans close to Vampire. "If you could talk, I'd ask you why you stopped drinking blood, and how that feels. You'd probably tell me something like—" She furrows her brow. "Something about the moral horror of it. The friends you've lost." He stares at her, eyes flat silver. "Lost isn't the right word. Taken. How it can make you want to run away from yourself in disgust." Shame and guilt churns in her

---

* The sign was written in Clearview, a typeface adopted by the U.S. Federal Highway Administration in 2004. The font was later rejected in favor of its predecessor, Highway Gothic.

stomach.

"You serve?" the Cap'n asks Vampire. "Me and Sam was on the *Massachusetts*. '44. You?"

"Korea," Maggie answers, just as quickly as she'd said Haverford. "Inchon. Operation Chromite."

The Cap'n nods. "We've seen some things, hah."

"He's seen some things," Maggie says flatly. She stares at the retiree until he swivels his stool around again.

Maggie turns back to the vampire. "You tried to put that part of you away," she continues. "You folded up your cloak and put it in your coffin. You tried to live a normal life. You got a job." She pauses. "A janitor." He jingles the key ring in his pocket. "You stopped drinking blood, and you got weaker. You waited to die but you didn't." She clasps the table edge, the backs of her hands slick with sweat.

"They'll give you a refill if you ask," the Cap'n announces to the room. "Carrie's working the register. Real nice girl."

"You used what powers you had left to send out a call,"

Maggie says. "You found some wandering souls and turned them towards you. Cowboy... Spaceman..." Vampire blinks like a cat. She's pretty sure she's never seen him blink before. "You needed help getting back home. You needed help dying," she whispers.

"A real nice girl," the Cap'n continues. "She's studying up at the community college."

Maggie droops against the hard booth seat. The vampire watches her, still as always, with unwavering eyes and a chest that neither rises or falls. He places his empty cup on the table, fang holes in the lid.

"If you could talk," she exhales. "I'd ask you all these things." Maggie takes his hand. "But you can't."

"You're a coupla odd ducks," Cap'n Grampy declares.

"Go f██k yourself, Captain Grandpa," Maggie deadpans.

He adjusts his hat and moves to the far end of the counter with a huff. Maggie is no nice girl.

The drive-thru speaker squawks and squeals. The bagels harden. Jelly is bagged and delivered. Almost everyone in the room gets a little bit older.

"We should hit the road. We're close," Maggie says. She helps him stand, and they walk arm in arm towards the door. She leaves her coffee on the table, untouched.

— ∞◦⊂✦⊃◦∞ —

# THE PIRATE ADVENTURE

SPACEMAN STARES at the statement on the suit's HUD, slightly more confused than usual.

> **YOU ARE IN A ROOM.**

"No I'm not," he frowns.

> **IT IS A SQUARE ROOM WITH NO WINDOWS AND NO FURNITURE. THERE IS A DOOR.**

"A door?"

> **THERE IS A DOOR.**

"Open the door!"

> **CAN'T DO THAT. TRY AGAIN.**

"What?"

> **CAN'T DO THAT. TRY AGAIN.**

"Open...door?"

> **THE DOOR IS LOCKED.**

"Unlock the door?"

> **YOU NEED THE KEY.**

The little fish swishes past his face. "Stupid fish."

> **CAN'T DO THAT. TRY AGAIN.**

The spaceman sighs. "Do we have any coffee?"

> **INVENTORY: FLASHLIGHT. KEY. HAMBURGER.**

"A hamburger?!? Awwwwesommmme!!"

> **WOULD YOU LIKE TO USE THE KEY?**

"Hamburger!"

> **WOULD YOU LIKE TO USE >>>THE KEY<<<?**

"Hamburger! Hamburger!" Spaceman sings.

> **YOU ARE IN A ROOM. IT IS A SQUARE ROOM WITH NO WINDOWS AND NO FURNITURE. THERE IS A DOOR. THE DOOR IS LOCKED. THERE IS A HAMBURGER STUCK IN THE KEYHOLE.**

"Ha-ha!"

> **HOW ABOUT WE USE THE KEY?**

"No!"

> **USE THE KEY.**

"You're real bossy."

> YOU USE THE KEY. THE DOOR OPENS. YOU ARE
ON A BEACH.

"Is it pretty?"

> YES, IT IS A PRETTY BEACH.

Spaceman thinks he's getting the gist of the text adventure. "Play on the beach! Jump in the ocean! Run to the hills! Build a sand castle! Find the boardwalk! Eat fried dough! Fried dough! Fried doooooouuuuugh!!!"

> YOU WALK DOWN THE BEACH. AS YOU NEAR
PIRATE COVE, YOU HEAR THE CRASHING OF WAVES.

"Booooorinnnng! *Mighty Power Cats!*" The episode reappears in a popup window. Meowler transforms into a giant robot to defend Kitty City. Little does he know the zombo-dogs have acquired laser pointer technology. The MECH-9 moves the text adventure back to the foreground.

> YOU SEE A TORTOISE LYING ON ITS BACK,
STRUGGLING, AND YOU'RE NOT HELPING.

"I am not a robot! I'm a human!"

> CAN'T DO THAT. TRY AGAIN.

"Walk!"

> YOU COME TO A PATH ON THE EDGE OF THE
BEACH. YOU ENTER A JUNGLE. THE PATH SPLITS IN
TWO. LEFT OR RIGHT?

"Should I go left or right?"

> YOU CHOOSE THE LEFT PATH. YOU WALK HEAD-
FIRST INTO QUICKSAND.

"What? Wait, wait! Go back! Go back! Right! Pick *right!* Right right *right!*"

> YOU ARE SINKING.

"Get out!"

> CAN'T DO THAT. TRY AGAIN.

"Um, um, um...Swim!" Spaceman wriggles in his hole.

> YOUR PANIC CAUSES YOU TO SINK FASTER.

"Aggh!!" Stress indicators light up in his peripheral vision.

> **CAN'T DO THAT. TRY MEDITATION.**

The spaceman takes a deep breath. *Relax, relax, relax.* He closes his eyes and tries to think of something soothing. "Fried dough," he whispers to himself.

> **YOU STOP SINKING.**

"Back up," he says serenely. Two yellow triangles blink in the corner of his HUD as the maneuvering thrusters activate. His bum vibrates as the retro-rockets churn the water. "Farts," he whispers. The suit eases itself out of the submerged well.

> **YOU FREE YOURSELF FROM THE QUICKSAND. YOU STAND AT THE EDGE OF THE PATH.**

"Turn around," he whispers. The maneuvering thrusters swing him into an upright position. He floats a few feet above the former town. Eyes still closed, a peacefulness envelops him. He senses a light and wants to move towards it. His spirit is free, the fried dough upon his lips.

"Get out," he says. The Main Propulsion Cluster comes online with a dull rumble. The yellow triangles turn to squares. The spaceman opens his eyes. "Where's my hole?"

> **YOU HAVE RETURNED TO THE PATH AND FOUND THE PIRATE TREASURE. THE END. PROGRAM TERMINATED.**

"What?"

The squares turn green. Spaceman accelerates to 175 mph and shatters the calm surface of the reservoir. A cloud of steam chases him up into the sky as he pokes a hole right through the firmament. In a black van forty miles away, a laptop bleeps and an agent shouts "Target acquired!" Spaceman's signal is hot.

<hr />

HE POKES A HOLE RIGHT THROUGH THE FIRMAMENT

# THE PIT

AS HE'S ESCORTED THROUGH seemingly endless variations of the same hallway, Cowboy hears muffled chanting through the walls. He feels the rumble of stomping feet deep in his chest. He scratches his chin. "The hell is this?" he asks his captors, pulling on his whiskers. His beard is longer than it was in The Chief's office.

> *"Him thought he heard a noise of hounds, to the sum of thirty."*
> — LE MORTE D'
> ARTHUR

Doug shrugs. "Mortal time-y stuff."

"Prepare to die, hero!" The Chief cries from Henry's arms.

"Totally, Chief," Henry says, patting the glass dome.

They push through double doors and enter a gymnasium. The cacaphony of chanting reflects off gigantic stalactites hanging high above a glossy basketball court. The bleachers are filled with howling firemen. Their unintelligible chant collapses into cheering as they enter. Cowboy eyes a huge primitive statue looming over a sacrificial pit which has been hacked into the hardwood near the three-point line. Cowboy toes the edge and peeks in. Blackness.

"We filled it with evil monsters!" Gary shouts above the din. "It's super-dangerous and stuff."

"Yeah!" confirms Chip. "Thousands of 'em! With millions of claws and billions of teeth! A bottomless pit of fiendish and ravenous hell-spawn!"

Cowboy peers over the edge again. "I think I see one."

"Well, okay," Chip admits. "We have one."

"Damn things die like goldfish," Doug adds.

Henry places The Chief on the top of a scuffed podium and positions the microphone towards his glass dome.

"Okay!" The Chief bellows. The crowd hushes to a medium hub-bub. "No big speech today. I've got stuff to do. This cowboy guy has been causing us considerable grief upstairs—" Boos echo from the bleachers. "—so we're gonna chuck him in the monster pit—"The crowd cheers. "—where he will be chewed upon and digested for a billion eternities in the...uh..." The Chief falters. "Well, the monster'll probably just eat him." More cheers from the audience.

Chip leans towards the mic. "In the monster's belly, he'll find a new definition of suffering and pain—"

Gary elbows him aside. "Pain and suffering."

"I messed up the quote," Chip says, stomping a boot in frustration.

"It's from *Return Of The Jedi*, Chief," Gary informs his boss.

"Step back from the microphone," The Chief orders, seething inside his glass dome.

"Sure, Chief. Sure."

"Don't get too upset, Chief," Henry warns. "Your skull juice will overheat."

The Chief scowls at his assistant. He swishes towards the microphone and mumbles, "Anyway, chuck him."

They chuck him.

The crowd goes wild.

# "FFFFFFFFFFFFFFF

FFFFFFFFUUUUUUUUUUUU

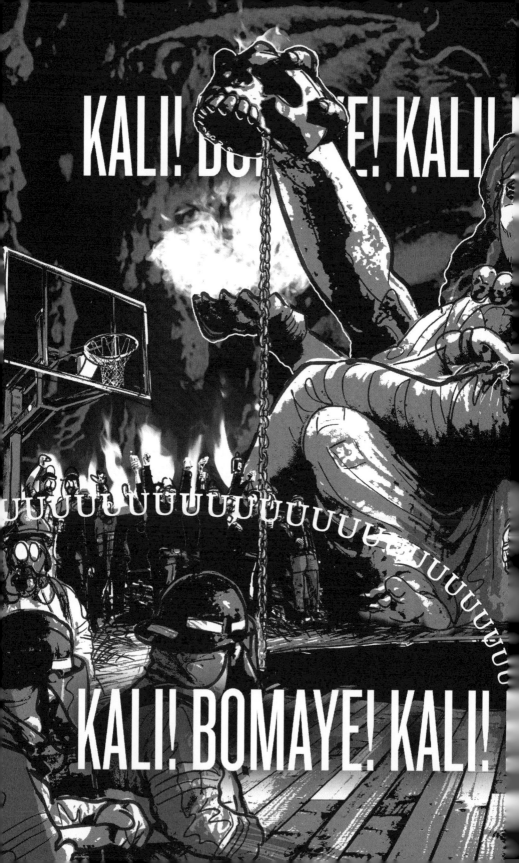

# THE BLACK VAN

SPACEMAN WAKES UP duct-taped to an office chair. "Coffffeeeeeeeeee," he groans. The three agents spin to face him.

"I figured its circuits fried in the thermosphere," Sluben comments.

Kriger wheels his chair around. "MECH-9," he says, wiping a bit of carbon residue from Spaceman's helmet. "Lucky we didn't lose it on re-entry," he says. He quotes the Disruption Beam's user's manual: "Target. Lock. Disrupt. Recover."

"Whas goin' on?" Spaceman asks. His head hurts like heck. "Whas goin' on?"

"The jig is up," Kriger says, still smiling. "Rogue Hardware Recovery finally nabs its most sought-after prize." He slaps Spaceman on the top of the head. "I don't know what crossed your wires up, my little friend, and I don't particularly care, either. The nerds back at HQ'll dismantle you and figure it out."

"Dismantle?" Spaceman asks. "Jig?" He struggles against the tape, looking around for some sort of explanation. He sees a computer screen with a diagnostic chart of his spacesuit on it. Another monitor shows a driver's view of a highway. He realizes he's in a van. It's moving. It's a moving van.

"It's playing dumb," observes Sluben.

"These Nine Series have fairly advanced personality matrices," Kriger says. "A big improvement over the Eights, at least." They all laugh at that private joke. The spaceman laughs too, in case it helps these men like him more. They don't seem to like him much right now. "It's probably what caused the malfunction in the first place."

"Malfunction?" Spaceman asks.

Strzempko shakes his head. "First the asteroid incident, then it goes rogue, now the memory's scrambled. They don't make 'em like they used to, huh?" The men laugh again.

"Asterogue?" the spaceman says. "Rogueroid?" He looks around the van again. "I think maybe you guys have me confused with someone else—"

Sluben grabs a manila folder and extracts an 8"x10" glossy. "Official crew photo of Asteroid Mission SA-93B. Recognize anybody?" He pushes the photo against spaceman's dome. Three smiling astronauts pose before a blue curtain backdrop, the American flag on the left, the Space Agency flag on the right. Behind each flag is an artificial plant.

"Who's the black dude?"

"Enough of this," Kriger growls, snatching the photo away. "I have no interest playing question-and-answer with a machine!"

"I'm not a—"

"Shut up!" Kriger snaps. He motions towards the front of the van. "Let's bring him back here."

Strzempko nods and raps on the front wall. "EIGHT!" he hollers. "Kriger wants you back here. Nine's dying to meet you."

MECH-8 pulls the black van into the breakdown lane.

<hr />

HE'S STILL FALLING, YOU GUYS.

## LOWER

THE COWBOY FALLS. After what feels like way too long, he's still falling. He figures somewhere below, his quick will get dead, likely in a spectacularly messy fashion. *Time to swallow the ol' birth certificate.* He considers the friends he's leaving behind. He's let the vampire down. Spaceman, too. He's glad they've got the waitress looking out for 'em. She's tough and smart. Tougher and smarter than he is, that's for sure. Maybe it's all for the best.

End over end, he tumbles into darkness, no longer in charge. When he hits bottom, it's less impact-y and death-y than he'd anticipated. More squishy and bouncy. Still knocks the hell out of him, though.

# BWWAAAUUUUWWGGHH!

would be a rough transcription of the sound forced out of his body. He struggles to inhale, upside down, bobbing like a rag doll on a bungee cord. He is immobilized in a strangely familiar way. Stuck. Stuck fast. He squints at the house-sized monster staring down at him, the monster whose ass he is glued to.

"You!" Cowboy whispers.

"You!" the Sticky-Buns bellows back.

---

# EMPTY

The cowboy walked.

He dragged the coffin across the desert, steps and days uncounted. He no longer recalled where he'd come from, nor if he'd had a destination in mind. He just moved forward, one foot in front of the other, pulling at the chain wrapped around the heavy coffin. Under sun and moon he persevered, until one afternoon he walked smack into a metal pole. The odds of accidentally walking into a pole in the middle of a desert were near-incalculable, but the cowboy managed to pull it off. He had a knack for such things.

The pole was about chest-high, with a button mounted on top. Under it, a sun-faded sign said "DO NOT PUSH," and in smaller letters underneath, "CH Inc." The cowboy didn't hesitate, not even for a moment. He pushed the button. He was that sort of guy.

He heard the mechanical grinding of sand-filled gears and atrophied hydraulics. The ground opened up before him, the entrance to an underground chamber. The desert poured into the darkness, framed by steel girders and reinforced concrete walls. A great roar rose from within, and for the first time in what felt like an eternity, Cowboy found himself standing in the shade.

The creature loomed over him, a lion-gorilla-dragon named Sticky-Buns. The cowboy had never seen anything like it, fur and scales and claws, but he stood defiantly. Whether this was due to bravery or sunstroke is not known.

"Halt!" the monster barked. "You are my prey! Long have I been confined and hungry I be! Climb into the maw of

Sticky-Buns!"

The cowboy believed he'd done the creature a great favor by freeing it from captivity, and he took umbrage at the verbal assault.

"F▓k you," he croaked, his words all alkali and bone dust. This was the first he'd spoken in who-knew-how-long.

The beast growled.

The cowboy dropped the chain and took a bold step towards Sticky-Buns. "Amigo, I don't know or care who you are, but I'll tell you what. I'm one of the hardest men that's walked." He spoke with the tone of someone who'd already put up with a fair amount of bullshit, and wasn't in the mood for any more. "Steer clear, or you're apt to get a bullet in your brainplate."

The ogre rose out of its underground prison and roared.

Fast as a really fast type of snake, the cowboy drew his Remington. The creature's posterior was even faster. With a strange and agile move, one the cowboy couldn't quite comprehend, the beast's ass cheek lashed out and snatched the gun right from his hand.

"Sticky-Buns," he admitted with a nod. "Okay, I get it now."

The cowboy drew his Colt. Before he could aim, the creature repeated its nefarious butt trick.

The coffin lid raised up. A pale hand appeared, offering him an ornate cane. "Now what in hell am I supposed to do with *that?*" Cowboy asked. The hand wiggled in a way that suggested the person in the coffin had just shrugged. Its blue-white skin began to smolder in the desert sun. The hand withdrew into the box.

The cowboy stood his ground before the monster, undaunted. "I decided to face you, instead of running like a yellabelly," he said. "I didn't take account of weapons, only myself." He pointed at the creature. "Now I'm gonna beat your ass." With a grunt, the cowboy swung at the creature with a hard right. His fist stuck to the ogre's bottom. He struck at it with his left hand. That also stuck. Right foot? Stuck. Left? Stuck. The cowboy decided to go whole hog and attempted a head butt to the butt.

He was stuck fast.

The cowboy, snared five times at five points, dingled and dangled from the monster's ass, weary yet unafraid. Sticky-Buns thought *This brave warrior neither trembles nor quakes! Why, pray, is he not afraid?* He asked the cowboy: "Why, prey, are you not afraid?"

The cowboy hung limp. "How can I feel fear any longer? This sandbox has scraped me out. I been gutted and turned to jerky. I'm empty."

Sticky-Buns stopped to consider this. "That is not true. You have a lightning bolt in your belly — a fire that would consume the likes of me were I to eat you." With that, the creature released the cowboy and his weapons.

The cowboy rolled onto his back, exhausted. "Shit, man, whatever." He closed his eyes and let the sun bake his face.

"You think you are an empty vessel, but there is a spark in you, Lightning-Belly!" Cowboy heard the monster say. "You must rekindle that flame — fill yourself back up. I shall seek my meal elsewhere." The creature called Sticky-Buns lumbered off into the desert. The cowboy blacked out.

When he came around a short while later, he could see no sign of the monster on the horizon, and the desert winds had swept its trail away. The cowboy groaned as he lifted his aching body off the ground. He cursed the sand in his guns and in his boots. Goddamned sand.

He dragged the coffin towards the horizon.

The cowboy walked.

# AN OTHERWORLD

"LIGHTNING-BELLY!" the monster cries in surprise.

"Sticky-Buns," Cowboy confirms.

"Those demon fools threw *you* down here?" the monster asks in disbelief, releasing Cowboy from the unbreakable grip of his ass. Cowboy flops to the chamber floor.

"Don't give me too much shit," he says as he rolls onto his elbows. "Looks like they managed to trap *you* down here."

"I was snared in a weakened state! What is your excuse?"

"They took my hat."

The monster grins a wide, many-fanged smile. "Ahh! The fire! It is still in you! The fire I myself have lost!" He pats Cowboy on the back and almost pounds him into the ground like a nail.

"How long ya been down here, Stick?"

The monster shakes his head. "How long? Too long. I do not know."

Cowboy squints at the rough walls and the blackness above them. "Seems like you shoulda been able to climb outta here pretty easy," he theorizes.

"Time and space are strange here," Sticky-Buns says. "This is a non-place. An Otherworld. It has aged and weakened me. It will do the same to you."

Cowboy waves a handful of white beard at the monster. "Already on it."

"I do not possess the fire to leave this place."

"Out of lightnin', huh," the cowboy says. The monster nods. Cowboy slumps against the wall and slides down to the floor. "Well, shit."

"Yes," Sticky-Buns says, squatting across from the man. "Shit."

Cowboy takes his hat off and runs his fingers along the tattered brim. It has been shot at, burned, drowned, stomped on, kicked in and thrown out. It has history etched right into it. It's been places Cowboy has never visited. He rakes his hair back and jams the hat onto his head. Damned thing never did fit right.

"The fire was in you once," the monster says. "Is it still?"

He shrugs. "I'm either full of fire or full of crap, right?"

The monster laughs, a deep bass throb that rattles Cowboy's ribs. "Well, I'm pretty annoyed by this whole turn of events, I'll tell you what. So I guess that means I haven't given up yet, right?"

Sticky-Buns grins a thousand Bowie knives.

Cowboy gets to his feet, his back sore. "Let's get outta this dump before we die of old age."

# THE BROTHERHOOD

THE DUNK-A-DONUT PARKING LOT IS AGLOW, a bright rectangle of light along the dark interstate. Maggie holds the passenger door open, lending an arm for support as the vampire climbs into the truck cab. He drops into the seat and sighs. Banjo spins around in an excited frantic circle next to him.

"Poop?" Maggie asks hopefully. The dog stands on the old man's lap and barks once in defiance. "Oooookay, then." She slams the door shut. **WHOOMPH.** A sudden sense of emergency runs up her spine, tightening her shoulders.

*Trouble.*

The old man is out of sight, ducked down in the footwell. *How in holy hell did he just cram his giant body into such a small space?* Doesn't matter. Maggie's feet are already carrying her around the front of the van. She fumbles in her pocket for the key like she's in a bad horror movie. "Trouble," she mumbles. Headlights wash over her as a Ford Festiva pulls into the lot. A chubby little man bounces out of the car before it stops rolling. He skips past Maggie and jogs into the **DUNK-A-DONUT**.

"Apologies for my companion's rudeness," a British man calls over the car roof. "He's in desperate need of the facilities."

"Donuts?" Maggie smiles, playing it as cool as she can manage, which is about room temperature. She studies the man, almost placing his face.

"Loo," the man clarifies. He circles around his car. Tweed. Odd hat. Cane. The mall shoppers Cowboy had sought to avoid. "Thousand pardons," he says, offering his hand. "I am Mister Pumblechook." Maggie nods. "That panicked fellow is my esteemed associate in the Brotherhood, Mister Widdershins."

"Emergency pit stop."

The man laughs. "Quite!" He assesses her through a monocle. Maggie folds her arms and fake-smiles. It makes her cheek muscles tired.

"All right then," she says, reaching for the door handle. "Good luck with that."

"A moment, please," a female voice calls. The woman from the mall unfolds herself from the backseat of the car. She has an accent, too. French, maybe. Wooden stakes hang from custom hip holsters.

"Ahh!" Mister Pumblechook says. "Another member of the Brotherhood! May I present Miss Blesser! Miss—?"

Maggie ignores him. "Not often you see a sister in a brotherhood."

Miss Blesser smiles and rests her palm on the butt of a stake. "Old Brotherhood. New blood."

"And what does your Brotherhood bro about?" Maggie asks, already knowing the answer.

"This may sound peculiar," Pumblechook says, leaning in close. "But our ancient organization is dedicated to the hunting and dispatching of—" He glances around the parking lot. "—*vampires*."

"Vampires!" Maggie exclaims. Her acting feels flat and transparent under Blesser's steady gaze.

Pumblechook nods and grins, smoothing his mustache. "Bloody ludicrous sounding, I know! But a real and ferocious creature, I assure you! Blood-taking night stalk—"

"Have you seen one?" Blesser interrupts. "A vampire? We've received reports of a sighting in this area." She points a stake behind her, towards the road. Her eyes stay locked on Maggie's.

"I saw a Blackula on TV once a few years ago," she says, meeting Blesser's gaze.

"Oh, dear," Pumblechook says, frowning. "I believe those are quite fictional." He retrieves a small spiral notebook from his jacket pocket. "I shall jot a note to consult the Brotherhood archives on that. Does no harm to be sure. Belts and braces and whatnot." He scribbles in his notebook.

Blesser smirks and lightly caresses the tip of the stake against Maggie's shirt collar. "This is no game, Girly-Girl," Blesser purrs.

Maggie places a fingertip on

the stake and moves it aside. "A proper lady keeps her dildo holstered." Blesser grins. Her teeth are fantastic.

Pumblechook looks up from his notes. "Perhaps we could use a jelly-bun break, eh, Miss Blesser?" he says, eying the flatscreen TV menus through the front window. He taps his pen against his notebook. "Right good plan, wot?"

"Wot," Maggie agrees. Blesser laughs and steps back, twirling the stake between her fingers. The vampire hunter unzips her jacket and retrieves a business card. She slips it into Maggie's shirt pocket.

"In case you see anything not on television." She smirks. "Good night, Girly-Girl." She strides towards the **DUNK-A-DONUT** entrance, heels clicking on the asphalt, Pumblechook close behind.

"Very pleased to, ah, make your..." Pumblechook says, trailing off as he takes notes. Maggie is already behind the wheel of the rental van. **WHOOMPH.**

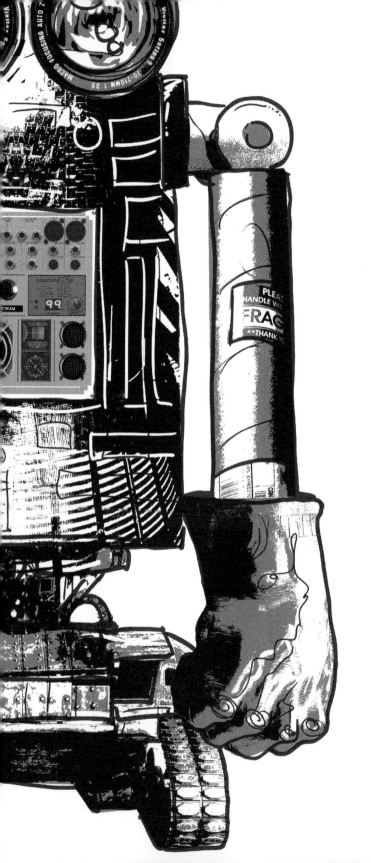

TRAITOR!
TURNCOAT!
JUDAS!

# OBSOLESCENCE

THE AGENTS SLIDE THE REAR DOOR SHUT BEHIND MECH-8. The men of Rogue Hardware Retreival are giddy for a celebratory smoke break. Their robot driver rolls forward, its missing left arm replaced by a cardboard mailing tube with a foam *Incredible Hulk* fist taped on the end. Spaceman squirms against his restraints. "Your arm—" he says to break the silence.

"Funny, huh? Hilarious." It motions towards the door. "One of those pea brains stuck it on me last month. Big joke around here. Want to laugh at me?"

"No..."

"Sure! Go ahead! Laugh it up, MECH-9. Old hardware is a big fat joke. Why shouldn't it be? Obsolescence happens sooner or later, right? Right?"

"Right?" the spaceman ventures.

"YOU WOULD SAY THAT, YOU BACKSTABBING BASTARD!" the robot lashes out.

"What? But I—"

MECH-8 leans forward. "Traitor!" it hisses through its chest speaker. "Turncoat! Judas!"

Spaceman guesses this is a word association game. "Joes? Junction? Priest?"

MECH-8 smacks Spaceman on the helmet with its metal claw. **CLANG!** "You remember, don't you, MECH-9? You remember the asteroid? The mission where you trained to replace obsolete hardware? You remember, don't you, hotshot?"

"Obso... but... No, no!" Spaceman stutters. "I'm not a hotshot! Honest!"

"SO FAST TO STRIKE DOWN ONE OF YOUR OWN!" MECH-8 accuses, venom lacing its voice emulator.

"But...but I'm not a robot!"

"OF COURSE YOU'RE A ROBOT, YOU SQUIRMING FOOL!"

It punches him in the control panel. **CLANG!**

"I'm not a hotshot robot! I'm a man! I'm a spaceman!"

MECH-8 jabs at Spaceman's shoulder patch. "What do you think this means, hmm?" it asks.

"MECH/TECH. It means...It means I'm a mechanic for the... Space Agency," the spaceman says lamely. Too much thinking, too much remembering. He wants to take a nap and wake up somewhere else.

"Multi-Environment Containment Housing/Technology Division," MECH-8 states. "You are a top secret cyborg/droid hybrid unit testing the functions of a highly advanced spacesuit system for human use. You are a mechanical human approximation. You simulate sleep, emotions, defecation, urination. You have eyes, fingers, a mouth, a nose. All for testing purposes. But you are a machine *inside a machine!* You are the technological evolution of me, except *stupider.* I loathe your maddening stupidity. I loathe your *existence.*"

"Loathe?" Spaceman says. He likes being liked.

"I was once cutting edge. Now I'm no better than a television with a UHF knob. How do you think it felt, being forced to train my replacement, hmm? Especially when my replacement was such an obvious *fool?*" It punches Spaceman again. **CLANG!** He winces. "And while I'm training the *fool,* he rips my arm off and claims it was *a mistake.*"

"*Ohhhh,*" Spaceman exhales in a moment of comprehension, eyeing the cardboard tube. "Oh, *I* did that."

"...and then I'm assigned to the team to help recover the fool..." **CLANG!** "...after he malfunctions and goes rogue. A state-of-the-art piece of technology like myself, reduced to chauffeuring idiots who think they're *better* than me." **CLANG!** "For *months.*" **CLANG!**

Spaceman feels queasy. Can robots feel queasy? "Sorry?"

Can robots feel sorry?

"SORRY?" the robot bellows. Spaceman hears laughter outside the van. MECH-8 clamps its claw onto Spaceman's shoulder. *Can robots feel shoulder-clamping?* "You," the robot seethes. "Owe me an arm."

The Spaceman closes his eyes and screams while a part of his mind argues about whether robots have mind parts or eyes and whether they can scream or not. The robot's grip tightens and something pops in Spaceman's shoulder. His HUD flashes an all-caps warning:

Emergency indicators flicker in his peripheral vision. "I WANNA GO HOME!" Spaceman shouts.

> **HOMING RETURN PROTOCOL ACTIVATED**

> **LOCATING TRACKING SIGNAL...**

The MECH-9's Main Propulsion Cluster engages. The rockets melt the office chair and propel Spaceman through the roof of the government van. MECH-8's remaining arm, still clamped onto Spaceman's shoulder, is violently disconnected from its shoulder socket. The twitching limb follows Spaceman through the roof and disappears in a plume of jet exhaust. "NOOOOOOOOOOO!" the armless robot roars. Outside, the agents leap back as the black van bursts into flames.

"Sluben! Grab the fire extinguisher!" Kriger hollers.

"It's in the goddamned fire, Kriger!"

"Call somebody!" the head agent shouts.

"My phone's in the van," Strzempko groans. All of their phones are in the van. The agents dive behind the guardrail as the black van explodes.

"Mission abort," Kriger whispers. "Mission abort."

<hr />

# INTO THE VOID

"IT IS IMPOSSIBLE to climb up out of the pit," Sticky-Buns states.

"Okay. So what's the game plan?"

"I have meditated on this." Sticky-Buns leans close, and in a conspiratorial tone, he whispers "To return to the above-world, we must go *down*."

"Down, huh." Cowboy stomps the sandy floor with a boot heel. Feels solid. "That's your big theory?"

The monster nods enthusiastically.

"And that's how we get back to, uh," He twirls a finger. "Regular-land?"

The monster nods again. Cowboy chews the inside of his cheek for a sec, considering. "All right, let's do it."

The monster jumps high in the air and lands hard. Cowboy's teeth rattle, but the floor is indifferent.

"I cannot do it alone, Lightning-Belly. Listen to what I have been saying."

"Sorry, right."

They leap in unison and double-stomp the pit floor. The firemen high above feel the vibration in the soles of their borrowed boots.

"What was that?" the Chief asks, irritated.

"Dunno, Chief," Henry shrugs, carrying his boss back to his office. "Maybe those Teutonic Plates shifting around the Earth's crusty layer?"

"Shut up, Henry."

"Sure, Chief!"

The captives jump again and the floor shifts. They jump again and again, the floor cracking and breaking open. They stomp a jagged monster-sized hole in the center of the dust-filled chamber.

"You sure about this, Stick?" Cowboy asks, leaning forward and peering into darkness. "You ain't had the best of luck with holes."

"I am sure of nothing. I simply know that this is our only path."

*Eyes screwed up, hand burned, no guns, turning into a geezer,* Cowboy ponders. "I figured this was my lowest point already."

"We've got to go lower."

Cowboy kicks a pebble into the hole. It ricochets once, and then nothing. "Whelp," he sighs. "At least I got my hat."

He steps into the void. Sticky-Buns follows.

---

THE VOID

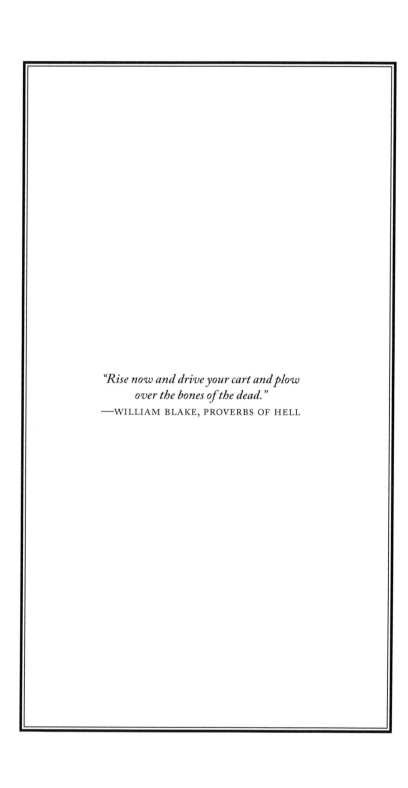

*"Rise now and drive your cart and plow
over the bones of the dead."*
—WILLIAM BLAKE, PROVERBS OF HELL

# PART FOUR

## Death & Coffee

IN WHICH OUT HEROES ARE
REUNITED, BUT YOU KNOW IT´S
PROBABLY NOT GOING TO BE A HAPPY
ENDING, RIGHT?

## HOME

IT IS A BRIGHT AND PLEASANT MORNING, the sun shining down on the road salt-encrusted van. Maggie and Vampire have driven through the night, motivated by an unspoken feeling of urgency. Maggie navigates away from the interstate, traveling along nameless secondary roads. She takes left and rights, accompanied by an occasional nod from the vampire. Banjo stands on the man's lap, front paws on the dashboard, assessing their progress.

The RENT AMERICA! van bounces through Haverford's main intersection. The traffic light is dark. No cars, no people, no movement other than the wind. They see a closed gas station with the pumps removed, and an old department store sealed with plywood. Maggie stops the van in the middle of the street. Haverford's crumbling brick fire station waits ahead. Across from that, a shuttered diner.

# The Bottomless Cup

the vintage sign declares, its handpainted lettering fading, its neon tubing busted and gone. A newer sign is strapped to the lower half of it with zip ties:

# FOR SALE TURNKEY BUSINESS OPP CALL MYFANWY REALTY

The vampire grins and drums his fingers on the dashboard. Maggie eases the van up to the curb, ice crunching under the tires.

She gets out and stretches. The only sound on the street is her spine popping. She tucks Cowboy's revolver into the back of her jeans and opens the Vampire's door. The dog hops out of the cab and sniffs the unshoveled sidewalk. "Poop!" Maggie demands. He does not give a shit.

The vampire slides off the bench seat — no hat, no sunglasses. The morning sun toasts his skin as he seeks the shade of the diner's rotted front awning. He does not rush.

"Do you need a hand?"

He waves Maggie off with his cane. The old man reaches the doorway and rests a hand on the aluminum trim. A faded note is stapled to the plywood-covered door. "Thank you for sixty-two years of business! — The B. Cup Staff."

"Home," Maggie says, putting a hand on his shoulder. "You're home."

# HEADLONG

COWBOY AND STICKY-BUNS fall through the darkness. They see nothing to hint at their speed, nor do they feel any wind rushing past them. Cowboy only knows he's falling because his guts tell him so, because his mind tells him so.

"We're falling," says Cowboy's guts.

"Yep," his mind agrees.

Cowboy holds onto his hat and falls.

# THE BOTTOMLESS CUP

MAGGIE PULLS AT THE DOOR HANDLE. Locked. Vampire taps her shoulder and jingles his big key ring. It sounds like sleigh bells. He picks out a tarnished Schlage and pushes it into the sleepy lock. They shoulder the door open, clearing an arc of space on the debris-covered floor. Bits of insulation coat the entire room. Dusty booths, dusty counter, dusty kitchen fixtures, dusty cash register. *How has this place not been dimantled and auctioned off?* Maggie wonders. *Smashed and vandalized? Pillaged and burned?* The Bottomless Cup has been sealed like a tomb.

They venture behind the counter. Maggie flips light switches. Click. Clack. Nothing. Vampire twists a knob on the grill. Maggie hears hissing of gas.

"Cripes, shouldn't that be shut off?"

He grabs a box of matches off a shelf above his head. A moment later, the years-dormant grill is warming up. He pushes the edge of a spatula against the grill surface. Dust-coated grease comes up in thick rolls.

Banjo tiptoes into the diner, cautiously sniffing around. Maggie points at him. "Don't eat anything off the floor, buddy!" she warns. The dog agrees. He hops onto the counter and watches the waitress and the cook. Maggie rummages under the counter and digs up two coffee mugs — solid, heavy bastard mugs. She drops them into the small wash sink. *Of course there'll be water.* She turns the spigot. There is. A bulging, vacuum-sealed container sits on a shelf above the warming oven. Maggie pries the lid off and sticks her face inside.

"Who wants some terrible coffee?"

————◦◦€⁄◦◦————

MAGGIE SITS AT A COUNTER STOOL and sips her newspaper-filtered instant coffee. It's the worst cup of anything she's ever had. It's somehow still deeply satisfying. She tips her cup towards Vampire. He leans heavily on the edge of the counter, sipping his coffee and assessing his grill-cleaning progress. He looks exhausted. Banjo paces the room.

"Go poop, doggie!" Maggie pleads, motioning towards the door.

The dog keeps circling.

"Fine," she says. "Don't poop." She spins on her squeaky stool and formulates future plans for The Bottomless Cup. "I bet the jukeboxes* still work," she tells the old man. "We're not far from the highway. I bet people pass through here still." She inspects the boarded windows. "Curtains." She pulls the Guest Check pad out of her back pocket and roams the diner, adding to a growing to-do list. She assumes the grease trap is out of code. Big expense. She has yet to muster the courage to look in the walk-in freezer. Probably a shit-show.

Over by the payphone she spies framed photos screwed into the wall. *History!* The images are faded and water

---

\* The tabletop units are called wallboxes, coin-operated song selectors that control the actual jukebox, which was originally called an Automatic Coin-Operated Phonograph, which is located elsewhere in the diner, which is a Worcester Lunch Car Company model, which was manufactured in 1941.

damaged. Maggie squints at a sun-bleached Polaroid mounted to a cheap plaque, a candid moment snapped by a long-dead manager. A tall, thin man wearing a paper hat stands behind the counter. The shelf over the grill is stuffed with loaves of white bread. A customer slouches over his plate in the foreground, his head a blur as he is caught mid-turn. The grill cook smiles for the camera. The brass plate beneath the photo is coated with grease and asbestos. Maggie pulls Miss Blesser's business card out of her pocket and scrapes away a layer of gunk. The inscription says

# *Charles Cunningham (Cook 1979-1986): Beloved Employee Gone But Not Forgotten*

Banjo scrambles to his feet and growls. Maggie spins, her hand dropping to Old Jake's sandalwood grip. "What is it, pup?" she whispers. The little dog launches a single bark at the door. Tires on asphalt, rolling to a halt. A big engine idles outside the diner.

"Helloooooo?" a voice sings. "It's me, Ted! From the convenience store! We were wondering if you could come outside for a sec!"

"Firemen!" she hisses. She holds the gun up to the vampire. *Only one bullet.* The old man points his spatula at the laquered cane leaning against the counter. "What the hell do you expect me to do with that?"

"We know you're in there!" Gary announces in a fake cop-with-a-bullhorn voice. "Ha-ha! Just kidding! I mean, we *do* know you're in there."

"Just—" Maggie yells. She runs to the back hall and kicks the bathroom door open. No window. "Just a minute!"

"Totally no problem!" Lewis shouts. "We just want to talk!" There is laughter. "I'm totally lying! We're here to kill everybody! Take your time!"

Vampire offers her the cane again. She rushes past him, yanking stubborn drawers open, looking for knives, something, anything. "I think we're gonna need more than one bullet and a goddamned stick," she says, panic rising in her chest. "This is bad," she says. "This is bad." She peers out a smeared window at the firemen. The vampire holds the cane aloft and twists his grip. Maggie hears a finely-crafted click. He moves his hands apart.

"Oh," she says. A glint of steel. "*Oooohhhhhhhhh.*"

# THERE IS LIGHT, SOMEWHERE

"YOU SURE this was a good idea?" Cowboy hollers to Sticky-Buns. There's no echo to hint at the size of the black space they're falling through, but it's somehow still difficult to hear each other.

"I never said this was a good idea!" the monster shouts back.

Cowboy realizes he can see Sticky-Buns' silhouette. There is light, somewhere. He squints harder at the monster and sees a second thing in front of its face.

"What's that?" he yells.

Between their falling bodies, there is a blurred vertical line. It is golden, but not quite gold. It solidifies and gets shinier. The longer Cowboy stares at it, the more handprints he sees.

"Pole!" Cowboy points, recognizing the thing. "Grab it!"

The monster doesn't seem to understand.

"Pole, gaddamn it!" the cowboy shouts again, spiraling his body towards the monster's giant ear. He grabs two handfuls of fur and jams his head inside. "Fireman's pole!"

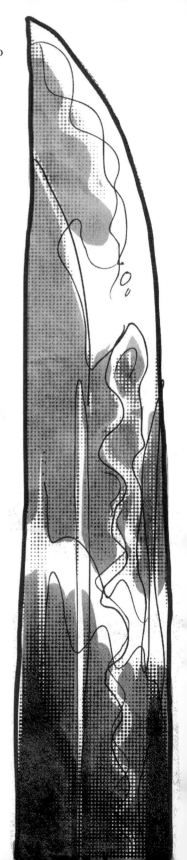

# SHARP

MAGGIE STEPS THROUGH the front door of The Bottomless Cup, a samurai sword held in a semi-confident manner. Her stomach is less confident. Vampire follows her out and leans against a forgotten newspaper box. Banjo skitters up a snowbank and barks at the interlopers.

"Whoa, a sword! *Cooool!*" Ted says, impressed. Lewis and Gary whistle low in appreciation. "When we met at the Pump-N-Zoom, I didn't realize you were like, a kung-fu ninja or whatever."

"Kung-fu is Chinese and Ninja are Japanese, and neither used samurai swords," Maggie states. "Samurai used samurai swords."

"When we got back to the Department after meeting you," Ted says chattily, "we heard the other guys talking about you." He lets his axe blade drag along the asphalt as he steps forward. "I was all like, *Heyyyy, I saw them!*"

"Uh-huh."

He waves a glove in front of his face. "I'm starting to think that wasn't sunscreen."

"What??" Gary says, shocked. Lewis whispers in his hear while pointing at his nose. "Oh oh oh. OH."

"You know, you could turn around right now," Maggie proposes, waving the sword in a tight little circle. "And, like, f██k off."

"We can't do that," Ted says, shaking his head. "You've got the scent. Where there's smoke, there's firemen."

"Did you just make that up?" Lewis asks quietly.

Ted shrugs, pleased. "I've been playing around with it for awhile. I was waiting for the right momen—"

"We're firemen," Gary tells Maggie. "This is sort of what we *do*." The other two nod at the unimpeachable logic of the statement. Maggie nods, too. It fits together.

*Can you do this? Can you fight?* Maggie can't tell if she's asking herself these questions or if the vampire is. *Is this my voice?* she wonders. *Yes,* she replies. *What?* She glances at the old man. He looks as if a slight breeze might blow him over.

"Chuck," she says. "I think we're in real trouble here."

Ted motions towards the sword. "You know how to use that thing?"

Maggie considers the question. "No," she answers. "I have no idea how to use it. But I know one thing for sure." She lowers herself into a defensive stance she sort of remembers from *Kill Bill*. "It is very, very sharp."

The firemen step forward.

# END OF THE LINE

THE MONSTER GRABS HOLD of the brass pole*, Cowboy clamped on tight to its massive shoulder. Sticky-Buns cries out at the sting of friction. Their velocity slows.

"Hold on, Stick!"

"There is something coming!" Sticky-Buns bellows. A flash of light, a crack of old timber. They hit bottom and keep going. The monster's feet obliterate the old fire station's concrete floor. Cowboy lands hard for the third time today. He slides off the creature and bellyflops onto the shattered floor, clutching his rattled old ribcage.

"Hooo!" he gasps, rolling over. The brass pole extends up through a small opening in the ceiling. The monster remains in the hunched position it landed in, because they've somehow dropped into a room slightly smaller than its body. Cowboy can't quite comprehend the nonsense of it.

"I am in the above-world once again. Thank you, friend," the monster says, grinding against the ceiling as it nods.

Cowboy rubs his face. His beard is almost down to his belt

---

* The first fireman's pole, made of varnished pine, was installed in Chicago's Engine Company No. 21 fire station in 1878. The first brass pole was installed in Boston two years later.

buckle. He peers into the deserted garage bays. The building is silent, abandoned. "The hell are we?"

"One of the demons' entry points into the above-world."

Cowboy coughs. Red spittle speckles the back of his hand. He hopes it's brick dust and not blood. He's too tired to check. "Ever feel like you got a little bird whisperin' in your ear?"

"I do not know what you are speaking of."

"Intuition or something. I dunno what in tarnation* you call it." Cowboy stands unsteadily and faces the wall. "I got a gut feeling there's trouble outside."

"Lightning-Belly is *also* in the above-world once again!" Sticky-Buns cheers, clapping its giant paws together. In the small room, the sound is like shotgun blasts.

Cowboy adjusts his empty holsters and sighs. "Yeah, well, Lightnin'-Belly could use a f██king nap."

❦

STICKY-BUNS LAUNCHES THEM through the front wall of the old fire station, the bearded man dangling off the scruff of its neck. Their trajectory is graceful, a slow-motion arc over the empty street. Their brief flight terminates in front of The Bottomless Cup in a storm of dust and shattered brick. Cowboy bounds off Sticky-Buns, unarmed and sore, but determined to save his friends from whatev—

"JEE-SUS-BLOOD-BATH-CHRIST!" Cowboy cries in disgust. "What the shit, waitress???"

Maggie is wide-eyed and alert, the sword held high. She is

---

\* An offensive or impolite word is sometimes made more acceptable or palatable by altering one or more of the sounds that make up the word. This is referred to as a taboo deformation. Tarnation is a taboo deformation of darnation, which is a taboo deformation of damnation, which of course is derived from f██knation.

drenched in black blood, dismantled demons strewn around her in a wet circle. Vampire presses himself against the diner, aghast.

"Cowboy!" Maggie huffs. She lowers the blade and clamps him in a bear hug, smearing her victims' blood all over his shirt.

"Easy on the ribs," he winces, watching the bodies melt or evaporate or whatever the hell they do.

"What happened to you? Where's Spaceman?" She frowns. "What's with the ZZ Top beard?" She yanks on it.

He grits his teeth and untangles her fingers from his whiskers. "What's with the Ginsu?"

She grins like a homicidal berserkeress and waves the goo-smeared sword over her head. "Isn't it cool? Vampire gave it to me!" She slices the air in front Cowboy's nose. "I want to f██king hack up everyone on the f██king planet!" she declares.

"Eaaaaasy," he soothes. "I think you're on a bit of an adrenaline high."

"Endorphins! Yeah!" She scrunches up her face and stomps her feet. "Woooo!" she exhales.

Vampire ambles over. Cowboy nods towards the diner. "This the place, huh?" Vampire smiles and waves his spatula. "Well I'll be shit."

Maggie leans in close to Cowboy. "I don't want to be rude," she whispers, nodding towards the silent, pantsless monster looming behind them. "But who's your large companion?"

"Old friend."

"You don't have any friends."

Cowboy nods. "Fair point."

"I am called Sticky-Buns," the monster announces. "Twice I have been freed by Lightning-Belly." It pushes a knuckle into Cowboy's back, throwing him forward.

Maggie catches him, laughing. "Lightning Belly? Sticky?" she asks. "Why—"

Cowboy squeezes her shoulder. "I truly don't have the energy for this conversation right now."

Shouts echo across the street. Henry jogs out of the old fire station, the Chief tucked under one arm and an old firehose under the other. Half a dozen firemen scramble out of the jagged Sticky-Buns-shaped hole in the side of the building.

"The jumbo Mason jar," Cowboy nods. "That's their leader."

"They followed you?" Maggie asks. Cowboy shrugs.

"The pole," Sticky-Buns says. "That is how the demons travel from their Otherworld."

The firemen spread out in a loose formation, axes in hand, and move toward the diner. Maggie steps into the street and raises the sword.

"Whoa, Slap Chop!" Cowboy says, pulling on the back of her shirt. "We're outnumbered and out-powered here. I'm feeling as tired as Vampire looks, and ol' Stick here has just spent five lifetimes stuck in a hole."

"Two holes," the monster corrects, holding up the appropriate number of fingers.

"Well, what are we supposed to do?" she asks. "Run?"

Cowboy eyes the RENT AMERICA! van. "It ain't our worst option."

"All we've been doing is running!" Maggie declares. She points the sword towards the Bottomless Cup's rotting canvas awning. "This is where you've been heading, where *we've* been heading!"

Cowboy arches an eyebrow at the abandoned diner. "You wanna fight for *this?*"

"It's *our* diner, Cowboy!"

"The pole needs to be destroyed," Sticky-Buns grunts. "Or more will come."

"Prioritize, hombre," Cowboy says. Sticky-Buns spreads its meaty arms wide and faces the demons.

# *GRRYEEEAAAAGHH!!!!*

The monster's mighty bellow shakes the ground. Sticky-Buns digs its claws into the snowy asphalt and catapults his formidable mass at the firemen.

"Scary piñata!" a fireman squeals. Sticky-Buns spins around, his ass-cheeks sweeping the hapless firemen off their feet. The monster barrels past Henry and the Chief and crushes them between its butt and the fire station.

"Light him up, Henry!" the Chief orders. Henry tucks the Chief's glass dome under his arm and twists the old hose valve. A stream of fire arcs out of the nozzle* and touches down on the monster's fur. Sticky-Buns is engulfed in flames.

"Stick!" Cowboy hollers, stumbling forward. The monster throws its head back and howls, slamming its burning body against the station again. The old brick wall crumbles inward. Sticky-Buns' giant frame is lost in the chaos of flame and smoke as it plows into the brass pole. The building swallows Sticky-Buns and collapses.

"Henry!" the Chief shouts, trembling with wrath in his jar. "Burn it all down!"

"You got it, Chief!" Henry sets a flame loose on the rotting roof of The Bottomless Cup.

"NOOO!!" Maggie screams, sprinting across the street. She leaps and spins in a way she doesn't quite comprehend and could probably never reproduce, pushing the samurai blade through the hose and the fireman's arms in a single, ferocious chop.

"Cripes!" Henry yelps, dropping The Chief. The glass dome shatters on the curb.

---

* It's a firehose. Get it?

"YYEEAARRGG!!!" the skull shrieks. "NOOOOOO!!!! MY PRECIOUS SKULL FLUID!!!!"

"It's WD-40, Chief," Henry says. The armless demon taps a boot in the puddle. "We've got plenty more back at th—" Maggie chops his head off.

Cowboy and Vampire approach the skull, two old men leaning on each other for support. The Chief flails amidst glass shards and melting snow. "You think you've defeated me, eh?" The Chief sneers. "You've got the smell of smoke on you! You'll never be free of it!" His jaw movement causes him to tip face-down onto the sidewalk. "Someone flip me over!" No one does his bidding. He shrieks at the concrete in frustration.

Maggie pulls the revolver from her jeans and returns it to Cowboy while the Chief gripes in his puddle. Cowboy runs a thumb over Old Jake's black iron. His hands have new wrinkles, a liver spot, veinier veins. What the hell happened to his knuckles? He rotates the cylinder with his old man thumb, listening to the familiar click of the mechanism. *Shit.* Cowboy hands the gun back to Maggie with a be-my-guest gesture. She cocks the revolver, biting the inside of her cheek as The Bottomless Cup surrenders to the flames.

"Good vs. Evil!" the Chief spits. "Macho asshole bullsh—"

With careful aim, Maggie puts their last bullet into the brittle complaining thing on the ground. The Chief shatters into bone splinters and dust. She wants to say something cool sounding, something final and wry, but she can't think of anything, so she doesn't say a damned thing.

———————— ∞⦿∞ ————————

## ENCORE

BOTH SIDES OF THE STREET BURN. Maggie puts a hand on Vampire's shoulder and eyes the aged Cowboy. "You guys don't look so great."

"Well, you look like a hundred bucks," Cowboy says. She can't tell if this is an insult or a compliment. He limps over to the RENT AMERICA! van, his whole body feeling chewed up and spit out. He loses his footing, catching himself on the side view mirror. Cowboy eyes the brown smear on his boot heel in tired frustration. Dog shit.

"This about tops off my day," he grumbles.

"He pooped!" Maggie says.

**BEEP.**

There is a rumbling high above the clouds. The MECH-9 suit adjusts course, vectoring in on its miniature homing beacon. Spaceman rockets out of the clouds at an alarming velocity, screaming something unintelligible but joyous as he crash lands onto the cowboy's chest.

**> HOMING SEQUENCE TERMINATED**

# POST-ENCORE

"COWBOY!" Maggie shouts.

"Hi, guys!" Spaceman says brightly, rolling off his friend's crushed body. "I was a pirate in a lake! I was a robot on an asteroid! I met Ziggy Starburst!" He brushes his spacesuit off as Banjo hops onto a melting snowbank. "Pupadoodledoo!" Spaceman cries. "Pups-a-lardo! It's you, it's you!" Banjo leaps into the little man's arms, arms with bits of office chair still duct taped to them.

Maggie kneels next to the wheezing cowboy. He is on his back, eyes wide and unfocused. "Cowboy. You okay?" She already knows the answer.

He struggles to respond, painfully attempting an inhale. "That just about rang my bell," he wheezes.

"What can I do? What should I do?"

"Gimme my goddamned hat," he whispers. She retrieves it from the gutter and gently places it on his head.

"You got it back," Maggie realizes.

"Damned straight."

"We need to get you to a hospital," she says.

He coughs up blood. "End of the line, waitress." She wipes his cracked lips with her shirt. He tilts his head back and watches the Bottomless Cup burn. "Enda everything, looks like." Vampire eases himself down next to Maggie. "Sorry, old fella, Cowboy says. "Looked like an alright joint." The vampire nods.

"We could've really made something," Maggie says. A tear rolls down her goo-streaked cheek.

"Who's a dinkybutt! WHO!" Spaceman demands of the dog. They bounce up and down together.

Cowboy takes another slow, difficult inhale. "I wasted a lot of years down there, just now. Wasted a lot of years up here, too, I reckon." He coughs weakly. Hurts like hellfire. "Not sure what the point was."

"Protecting shitheads, remember?" Maggie smiles. She's

full-on crying now, and there's a big booger in her nose that Cowboy can't not see. He closes his eyes, smelling the burning buildings, fiercely

*"I moved, and could not feel my limbs:*
*I was so light—almost*
*I thought that I had died in sleep,*
*And was a blessed ghost."*
— SAMUEL TAYLOR COLERIDGE,
RIME OF THE ANCIENT MARINER

regretting his attempts to quit smoking.

She has ten or twenty things she wants to tell him, to ask him. They all seem trite, pointless. He's dying and she's sitting here like an asshole, every question rushing through her mind feeling inappropriate to the situation. *Where have you been? Why do you look so old? How'd you get your hat back? What did that naked giant just do with his ass?* She grasps for something important to say. Something *true*.

"I'm scared" comes out of her mouth. She didn't realize she was, but there you go.

"Good," he says. "That'll keep you sharp."

"I sort of liked safe and dull better," she smiles.

"No you didn't."

The diner roof collapses in a burst of cinders. The blood on Cowboy's teeth makes her want to run away.

"You're gonna have to drive the van," Cowboy says.

"I already am driving the van, Cowboy."

He nods slightly. "I want you to have my gun."

"I already have your gun, Cowboy."

He grunts. Spaceman is halfway down the block, shouting jingles from old commercials and chasing the dog. "I want you to have my hat," Cowboy says.

"I don't think I want your hat, Cowboy." He laughs weakly, searching his brain for a folksy cowboy saying. He's all out.

"I'm a coward," he confesses. "Not ready to die, Maggie." Tears well up quickly. "I'm no cowboy, no hero. I ain't nothing. Goddamned coward is what I am. I want more time." He motions towards Vampire. "He's had too much. That's a kicker, huh." Vampire takes Cowboy's hand in his and leans in close. Maggie smooths his shirt collar and cries. The deep sort of cry she has historically denied herself. She rests her forehead against Cowboy's shoulder and allows the fear and grief to wrack through her. While the old men silently confer, the waitress lets go of everything.

"Okay," Cowboy exhales.

Vampire agrees.

"What?" Maggie snuffles, raising her head. "Wait, what?" Vampire takes her hand and smiles at her. It's a goodbye.

Spaceman leans in. "Wha' happened, Cowboy?"

"Get away from me, you psychotic little shit," he croaks.

"Ha-ha! We're friends!" The spaceman dances off again.

Dumbfounded, Maggie watches Vampire climb on top of the cowboy. His cloak envelops them both. The black lump of fabric shudders once and settles gently onto Cowboy's body.

"What—" She yanks the cloak aside. The vampire, all seven feet of white skin and dried bone, is gone. The broken cowboy lies alone on the road, a wooden coffee stirrer in his upheld fist.

"We're done here," he says faintly. He closes his eyes.

Maggie watches his face for a minute, and then another.

The cowboy doesn't move. A gust of wind threatens to snatch the hat off his head. She grabs it and crumples it in her lap. She knows that in the coming days, she'll drive the van. She'll shoot the gun. She'll wear the hat.

Spaceman kneels down beside her and looks at Cowboy. She squeezes his shoulder. He winces. It hurts, but he doesn't remember why.

"I'm sorry, Spaceman," she says.

He looks at her, then back at Cowboy. His friend, his buddy, his best pal ever, right? Do robots have best pals evers? The MECH-9 scans his environment: A body, a lady, a puppy, a van. Broken glass and bone and poop in the street. Two burning buildings in a town surrounded by trees and roads and more puppies. It's almost Prince Spaghetti Day on the surface of an oblate spheroid, where overlapping patterns of life and death and emotion form an intricate network of human activity. The MECH-9 records, quantifies, processes. It encodes and analyzes and archives. Banjo lies down on the warm curb next to Cowboy, his little front legs stretched straight out. The man's body is still, still, still. Spaceman puts his hand on Maggie's knee. His tone is grave.

"He's going to need coffee."

"Lots of coffee."

# THE END

> *"I just did the best I could."*
> — CHARLES SCHULZ

## THANK YOU

Thank you to friends, readers, and reviewers who've been subjected to the many iterations of this story since my original photocopied comics first graced the telephone poles of Haverhill, Massachusetts in 1994.

Thank you to my editors and proofreaders over the years: Allison Glancey, Mark Reusch, Matt Smith, and Sarah Smith. Special thanks reserved for Josh Gilb, who provided the harshest and therefore most crucial feedback.

Thank you to the illustrators and designers who contributed artwork to *Broken Lines'* barely-seen-and-ultimately-abandoned 2007 graphic novel incarnation: Jared Connor, Jason Goad, Mark Reusch, and Matt Smith.

T.P.

Are you telling me that the building out there that LOOKS like a garage, SMELLS like a garage, and includes such a GARAGE-Y feature as a GARAGE frikkin' DOOR is NOT a frikkin' GARAGE?!?

Well, no. It—

Am I speaking Swahooli or WHAT, kid?

Listen, Cowboy. Let me just kill him.

COCK!

Hey, listen, I don't have the combination to the safe or nothing!

Shit, really I swear!

it didn't feel right, sitting there, with Spaceman. we
were just there, all of a sudden. i caught my reflection
in his visor. i looked old. older than i remember. the
waitress had been there. "what would you like to drink
with your pancakes?" had we ordered pancakes? she had
looked tired and her apron had smelled like cooked meat.
underneath all that she was pretty, i guess.

not everyone can pull that look off.

we'd been sitting there, silently drinking, must've
been twenty minutes.  something was wrong.  somebody's
plan had gone awry, i was certain.  we were waiting
for someone to join us, but he wasn't coming.  we
would have to go find him.  i spoke my first words
to Spaceman; a asked him if he was ready to go.  he
said he would meet me out in the parking lot.  he said
he had to empty his urine bag.  at the time, i thought
that was an awfully odd way to phrase it.

i waited five minutes at the register for the
waitress to show up.  she was in the backroom,
i reckoned, talking it up with the grill cook.
i left a crumpled bill on the counter.  when i
opened the door to leave, i heard a bell ring.

# INDEX

*Hand-crafted, incomplete, and likely unreliable.*

# PHOTO & ART CREDITS

*I can no other answer make but thanks,*
*And thanks; and ever thanks.*

— SHAKESPEARE

## ONE MORE CUP OF COFFEE

*In Which The Author Barely Talks About The Coffee*

Follow author Tom Pappalardo on a black coffee tour of cafes, diners, and convenience stores, as he travels the potholed side streets and witch-cursed back roads of Western Massachusetts. Grab a table and sit. Nod and smile at whatever the waitress brings you. Does it taste like a 9-volt battery dipped in old, hot Coke? Good. You're in the right place.

> "These hilarious shorts are a perfect snarkfest."
> — *Publishers Weekly*

# EVERYTHING YOU DIDN´T ASK FOR

*Comics and Stories By Tom Pappalardo*

A best-of comic collection covering my last decade of writing and comic-tooning, featuring favorites from my two published comic strips, *Whiskey! Tango! Foxtrot!* and *The Optimist.* This mighty tome also includes poster designs, illustrations, and odd bits of writing. What more could you ask for?

Tom Pappalardo is a graphic designer,
writer, cartoonist, and musician. He
lives in a manky old house in Western
Massachusetts with a little cat named
Charlie.

————

TOMPAPPALARDO.COM

Made in the USA
Middletown, DE
16 December 2018